A DIFFERENT LIFE

He poked at the coals. . . . Up until now he had always lived free and open at Ruby Canyon, with no greater worry than the thought that his roof might leak in a big rain. Now he had to think about sleeping with a pistol under his pillow and a plank propped against the door. . . .

He couldn't assume O'Leary had made this move against him, but there was a good chance he was the one. And a fair chance he wasn't. Henry wasn't even sure whether it was a man or a woman.

As he rode to town, he was engulfed in sadness he at first did not understand. Then he realized he had lost something in this new turn of events. He had lost the freedom to go about his daily life without worry. Life had been open, without fear of his fellow man; now it was closed, tainted by suspicion. It was as if something had died, as if the bloom had gone and would not be back.

Other *Leisure* books by John D. Nesbitt:
ONE-EYED COWBOY WILD
BLACK DIAMOND RENDEZVOUS

WILD ROSE
of
RUBY CANYON

JOHN D. NESBITT

LEISURE BOOKS   NEW YORK CITY

For my brother David

A LEISURE BOOK®

May 1999

Published by arrangement with Walker Publishing Company.

Dorchester Publishing Co., Inc.
276 Fifth Avenue
New York, NY 10001

ISBN 0-8439-4520-6

The name "Leisure Books" and the stylized "L" with design are trademarks of Dorchester Publishing Co., Inc.

Printed in the United States of America.

WILD ROSE

of

RUBY CANYON

CHAPTER 1

AS HENRY SOMMERS rode up toward his dugout cabin, he could see the wild roses blooming from a hundred yards away. They were pink and bright in the warm afternoon sun, and Henry smiled as he made mental note of the date. It was the twenty-sixth of May. He had watched the pointed scarlet buds forming in the last couple of days, and now some of them had opened.

In the half dozen years he had been in Wyoming, he had gotten to know the country from its broader features down to its smaller ones, and it took some attention. The wild roses bloomed a little while after the meadowlarks came back and at about the time the rattlesnakes came out. In past years, Henry had seen the roses bloom a few days earlier in May, and he had seen them hold off until June. He had seen them last for only a week, and he had seen them bloom for over a month. No two years were alike in the way the calendar and the weather went together, but he couldn't remember a year when the roses didn't bloom at all.

Spring came slowly to the northern plains, and much of what was called springtime would pass for winter in other places—sleet, late wet snow, hovering rain clouds. When the wild roses bloomed, the warmer weather was making more of a show. A fellow could ride out, as he had done today, wearing only a light denim jacket with his gloves in the pocket. It was a time of promise, with grass greening up and the trees leafing out. There was always a chance of another cold, wet spell, but the warm weather was setting its feet down. Henry's horse Beau was all done shedding,

1

and the warm sun on the brown horse's neck and withers brought a smell that belonged to just this time of year. All of these things together—the color of new green, the angle and warmth of the sun, the texture of the air, the smell of horsehair—they all added up to a sense of late spring, with early summer not far away.

Those were the signs, also, that it was time for spring roundup. In a few days, Henry would go back to the Box Elder Ranch to gather, rope, and brand for Cyrus Blaine. Henry had gone back on the payroll in April, and now that there were a few slack days, Cyrus had given him some time off to come look after his homestead at Ruby Canyon. Once he was on roundup, there would be no more days off for six weeks or more. By the time he came back again, the wild roses would be long out of bloom, and the afternoon shadow in front of the cabin would have moved south and started back north again.

Beau came to a stop at the edge of the shadow and stood relaxed in the sunlight as Henry swung down. He patted the horse's neck and squinted at the sun. It was still high and warm. Over the next three hours the shadows would creep out; then the sun would slip behind the rim, and the air would chill.

Henry looked around behind him. He had ridden from the southeast, where he had been out to look at the country. His own quarter section was a small parcel in the broad expanse of plains, much of which was still open range, broken here and there by ranch headquarters or by small settler claims like his own. This big country seemed to stretch forever in every direction. A traveler moving across might think there were no boundaries and no center, but if a person had a place to belong to, then the rest of the world reached out from there. For Henry Sommers, the center of the world was his homestead claim of a hundred and sixty acres with a cabin in the northwest corner, at the base of Ruby Canyon.

People who didn't know the country would say the plains were flat, but anyone who had to make his own way on foot or on horseback knew that even the flattest country was anything but level. It was full of dips and rises, draws and hummocks, even in the flattest spots. A man might be able to see a bunch of cattle two miles away but miss another bunch that was within a quarter mile. Because the landscape changed with every step, a fellow needed to be watching it all the time.

Henry's hat brim cut the glare as he scanned the country. He thought he saw a rider to the east, and then the speck dropped out of sight, like a fly in a rumpled gunnysack. Henry relaxed his eyes, let them rove to the south and back to the north, and then looked across the rippling grey-green prairie to the east. The speck reappeared, larger now. It was a man on a horse, headed toward the dugout at Ruby Canyon.

As the horse and rider came closer, Henry could see the bay horse had a narrow blaze that went halfway to the nose. Otherwise, there was nothing remarkable about it or the rider at a distance.

They had come within a quarter mile of the cabin when the man raised his right hand to wave, and then the horse began to buck. After a few pitches the bay leveled out and broke into a gallop toward Henry and the cabin. At about a hundred yards out, the rider yanked the horse to a stop. Then he moved it forward in a walk. As the rider approached, Henry thought the man looked like Van O'Leary. He hadn't recognized O'Leary sooner because that wasn't the horse Henry's neighbor rode the few times Henry had seen him. And he hadn't been able to make out O'Leary's red hair, the man's most obvious characteristic, until he came within closer range. At fifty yards out, the man waved and then continued to walk the horse into the yard. He put both his hands on the saddle horn as the horse came to a standstill.

"Howdy," O'Leary called out.

"Good afternoon," Henry called back.

O'Leary moved the horse in closer, and as he dismounted he said, "Been by here a couple of times and never found no one at home. Looks like I caught you today."

"That you did." Henry moved Beau's reins to his left hand and stepped forward to meet the visitor.

The two men shook hands. As they did, Henry felt the small nag of guilt that he should have recognized the man sooner, so he took a good look at him. O'Leary was about the same height as Henry or perhaps an inch shorter, and he had a medium build. He was probably in his late twenties. He had red hair and blue eyes, half a week's stubble, and a friendly smile. His hat was sweat-stained and his clothes were worn and dirty, as a working man's might be.

"I didn't recognize you at first," Henry said. "I suppose it was the horse."

O'Leary smiled and then waved his head in the direction of the bay. "Oh, yeah. He's a new one. I got him from a new fella named Windsor, over south of here."

"Did you trade your sorrel?"

"Nope. Just made a straight deal on this one. I didn't like the idea of bein' limited to just one horse. He goes lame on you, an' then you're stuck. Especially livin' out where I do."

"Uh-huh." Henry recalled O'Leary's place out on Crow Creek, which he had visited once. It wasn't any more isolated than the other homesteads that had popped up here and there, but to a newcomer it could seem that way. Most people who had livestock to work—or ground to till—had more than one horse anyway, but O'Leary was just getting started.

"And of course, Dora can ride old Sam."

"Well, that's good." Henry had met Dora the last time he saw O'Leary, who had invited him to dinner. He could picture her now—a small-built, light-featured woman. It was an agreeable picture.

From an inside pocket of his jacket, O'Leary drew out a leather pouch that Henry recognized from before. Holding it in his left hand, O'Leary raised the flap and doubled it back, then with right thumb and forefinger lifted a sizable pinch of dark, stringy tobacco. As he motioned the pouch toward Henry, who shook his head, he poked the tobacco into his mouth and moved it to his left cheek. He spit on the ground and then spoke.

"Yep. Like I said, I been by a couple of times here lately, but this is the first time I've found anyone home."

Henry felt nettled at something he couldn't identify, but there was really nothing private about his comings and goings, so he said, "I've gone back to work at the Box Elder. We've got just about everything ready to roll for spring roundup, and the boss gave me a couple days to come and look things over."

"Well, I don't want to keep you from your work."

"Oh, nothing pressing. Just a couple of little things I wanted to get done. You know how that is."

"I sure do. Is it anything I can help you with?"

"Oh, no. But thanks. It's just little things."

O'Leary looked around as he stuffed the pouch back inside his jacket. "Always somethin', isn't there?"

"Seems like it. Especially when I'm not here all that much."

"Probably worse when you are. Work just seems to pile up when you're there to see it every day."

Henry gave a short laugh. From the little he knew of O'Leary, the man seemed very much in the style of the old boys who liked to sit around and chew tobacco, whittle, and talk about their coon dogs. O'Leary had said he was from southern Ohio. From the general air the man had about him when he dipped himself a pinch of tobacco, there was the sense that work waiting did not mean work pressing. And for as much as a person in this country appreciated an occasional visitor, Henry didn't feel like dawdling in O'Leary's style when he had work to do that he had planned to get done that day. "I suppose," he said.

O'Leary shifted his weight and moved the reins back to his left hand. "Well, I shouldn't keep you. Main reason I dropped by was to tell you I was plannin' to go into town this evenin', and I wanted to stand you to a drink."

Henry's thoughts flickered. It was a Saturday. He hadn't been to town for a while, and the evening would be a better time to chew the fat anyway, so he said, "Sounds all right. I'd guess you're goin' by yourself."

O'Leary grinned, showing tobacco juice between his lower teeth. "Man's gotta get out on his own once in a while," he said, "and keep in touch with the rest of the world."

When O'Leary was gone and Henry had gotten Beau into motion, he thought about the visit he had just had. There was something that had made him uneasy, and he was trying to pinpoint it.

He hardly knew O'Leary, had talked to him only twice. The day they met, the red-haired man had ridden up to Henry's place and introduced himself. He had complimented Henry on his dugout, or "shanty." After he had gotten a clear idea of what land was Henry's and had found out where Henry worked, he had invited his new acquaintance to come have supper the next day at his homestead on Crow Creek.

Henry recalled his visit to the O'Leary place. It was a homestead that had already been claimed and proven up on by a man from Indiana. He had built a clapboard cabin and a rough lumber shed, ripped up forty acres of range land to plant wheat, gone broke in two years, and sold out cheap. The forty acres had gone to weeds, but the house was still livable.

The visit had been pleasant enough. Dora O'Leary had fixed fried chicken, mashed potatoes, and gravy, which was something of a compliment to the guest, as the O'Learys had not yet gotten their own chickens or spud patch and had evidently gone out of their way to serve a nice supper. Dora was a friendly, hospitable woman, and Henry remembered thinking as he rode home that O'Leary was a lucky man. After that visit, Henry had begun to think more deliberately that a woman—though not exactly that same cut of a woman—would make the cabin at Ruby Canyon into a home.

Today's visit from O'Leary struck Henry as a little strange. His neighbor was still easygoing and cheerful. Nevertheless, there had been something irritating beneath the surface of the conversation.

Henry wasn't really bothered by the knowledge that O'Leary had been dropping by in his absence. He did have the sense that O'Leary had looked the place over pretty thoroughly, but that was all right. Henry always left his place on its own, and he wouldn't lock the cabin if he could. The code of the country was that if someone happened by in a snowstorm or thunderstorm, he was welcome to hang his hat and weather it out. Because of the distances between folks and because of the weather, things just about had to be that way.

No, there was something else, Henry thought. It had something to do with his not recognizing O'Leary soon enough. Uh-huh. It was the bay horse. It seemed like an odd thing for O'Leary to buy at this point, when he was just getting started. The average nester would have chickens and a milk cow first, and make sure he had a truck patch started. Then he would get a work horse or two to put in a crop and to work any cattle he might get together.

But an extra riding horse at this point seemed out of place. Henry shrugged and told himself it was none of his business.

Then he recalled that O'Leary hadn't said what kind of a deal he had made for the horse or whether he had even paid for it yet. Henry shook his head and told himself it still didn't matter. For his own part, he had firewood to gather, and it was work enough for him and Beau to go up the canyon and drag back a few dead snags.

Henry and his horse made three trips, dragging back a dead cedar tree, a cottonwood limb, and a small dead tree that Henry did not recognize. At this time of year he didn't need a great deal of firewood, but while he had a little time he liked to lay in a supply. It was good to have a selection of different sizes—he would have pieces ranging from small sticks to thick chunks. In addition, he would have more than one kind of fuel to choose from. He liked cedar the best, for the aroma it gave off as he cut it and for the combination of fragrance and long-lasting coals when he burned it.

Some cowhands didn't like to work with an ax—or with any long-handled tool, for that matter. A good many of them were Texas hands who had come up the trail, but the attitude was contagious with young men who came from the East to be cowboys. Henry, on the other hand, had grown up in a family that believed all work was good work, and now that he had his own place, he was glad he had always been on friendly terms with the shovel, the hoe, the pitchfork, and the ax. While some men complained that a shovel or a pitchfork gave them blisters, Henry had had callouses for as long as he could remember, and they came back every year.

As he went to get the ax, he passed the clump of wild roses. He paused and smiled as he looked at them. A couple of petals had already fallen to the ground, but there were plenty of other dark buds that would bring on fresh blooms. As he stood there in the quiet of the vast country, the sharp, clear tink-a-link of a meadowlark came across the fragile spring air. He looked around until he located the bird, perched on the peak of the dugout. The bird fluted again. It was a happy sound, the song of life springing anew on the western plains.

Henry fetched the ax and went at his work. It was clean, vigorous labor, and it made a fellow feel good to have the muscles warm and the blood pumping. When he stopped for a breather he could hear the sound of Beau munching grass, shifting his hooves, and dragging the picket rope. During one rest he heard again the silver call of the meadowlark, and he looked for the bird. It had moved. Then it sang again, and he looked at the wild roses, smiling with promise. In that moment he knew it was great to be alive, in the center of the world, here on his own piece of ground at Ruby Canyon.

CHAPTER 2

OF THE THREE saloons in the town of Willow Creek, the Gold Eagle had the most night life. Although O'Leary hadn't specified a place, Henry imagined the Gold Eagle would come closest to his idea of keeping in touch with the rest of the world, so he headed there first. Night was just falling as he rode up the street, and he recognized the bay horse at the hitch rack. He tied his own horse at an open spot a few horses down.

Right away he spotted O'Leary, who had a bottle of whiskey on the bar in front of him. When he saw Henry walk in, he called for another glass.

"I see you got away all right," Henry said as he took a seat at O'Leary's right. Then, accepting the glass that came his way, he said, "Thanks."

"My pleasure," O'Leary answered. He set the bottle midway between them and said, "Yeah. I made my escape. It's somethin' a fella needs ever' now an' then." He smiled, gave two light nods, and then turned away to his left and shot a stream into the spittoon.

They made small talk for a while. Henry didn't have any uppermost ideas to work over, and O'Leary didn't seem to, either. The talk drifted onto the topic of opportunity, and O'Leary said the western country offered great possibilities, especially to young men their age. He went on to emphasize it was even more so for someone like Henry, who worked hard. "You're the best kind," he said. "You hold down a reg'lar job, and you work up your own place, too."

Henry didn't have a ready response for such direct praise, so he said nothing.

After about a half minute of silence, O'Leary spoke. "I said fellas our age. Who d'you think is the oldest, 'tween you and me?"

Henry shrugged. "I'd guess I am. You tell me. I was born in 1861."

"Well, then, you're a year older. I was born in 1862. The day Van Buren died. That's why they named me Van." O'Leary's cheek bulged as his jaw moved sideways. "Me, I'm more for the present. If I had a son right now, I'd name him Grover, while the man's still in office."

Henry nodded.

"Fact. I would."

Henry smiled.

O'Leary spit again into the spittoon. "What do you think?"

"Oh, I think I would have guessed you a few years younger."

"Lotsa people do."

The talk went on as before, with O'Leary praising the railroads and the water projects for making it possible for the little man to make it. His tongue seemed to be a little looser, and his words a little more rounded off, than Henry had noticed before. But he obviously had been home for a change of clean clothes, so he hadn't ridden directly from Henry's place to the Gold Eagle. Judging from the amount of whiskey gone from the bottle, Henry imagined O'Leary had gotten there about an hour earlier.

When there was a pause in the conversation, Henry asked if everything was all right out on Crow Creek.

"Oh, yeah."

"Wife all right?"

"Oh, yeah. I told her I was comin' in to see you, and she thought that was just fine."

As the conversation moved on and the saloon began to fill up with more people, Henry noticed O'Leary glancing around from time to time. Then at one point, while

O'Leary was turned toward Henry, a man came up behind O'Leary and laid a hand on his left shoulder. As O'Leary turned to see who it was, Henry saw the man more clearly.

The first thing he noticed was a silver Vandyke beard, which was neatly groomed, and a clean gray hat. The stranger had light-colored eyes and reddish blond hair, with silver showing at the temples. He had a half-smile on his face but had not yet said a word.

O'Leary turned around a little more and stuck out a hand. The stranger's hand left O'Leary's shoulder and met for the handshake. By now the crowd in the saloon was loud enough that Henry did not overhear what the two men said, and as a matter of common courtesy he gazed away at the set of elk antlers behind the bar. Then, still trying not to eavesdrop, he turned to his own drink.

A movement and a sound caused him to look back around. The stranger was laughing, with his mouth open and his head thrown back. It was a high, loud, forceful laugh—the kind of nervous laugh that some men seem to carry around with them and can produce at any moment.

Henry turned to face his drink again. After a couple of minutes, a movement at the edge of his vision caught his attention. As he glanced around he saw the clean hat moving away. Henry gave O'Leary an inquisitive look.

"Windsor," said O'Leary. "He was just passin' through, or I'd've introduced you."

"That's all right," Henry answered, remembering he was the man who had sold O'Leary the bay. "I can meet him some other time." Then he wondered if O'Leary had felt any uneasiness at the meeting. Sometimes, if a man owed money and then met his creditor in a saloon, a cloud of guilt might hang in the air for an instant, but Henry didn't sense any such feeling at the moment. Nevertheless, from the way that Windsor had laid his hand on O'Leary's shoulder, Henry had the impression that O'Leary owed him or was in some way subordinate. Maybe the laughter was

WILD ROSE OF RUBY CANYON ■ 13

meant to help lighten the moment. Henry looked beyond
O'Leary and saw Windsor walk up to a saloon girl and tip
his hat. "I can see why he didn't want to waste any time,"
Henry said.

O'Leary turned around. "Well, damn him. He's a reg'lar
hound dog. I don't think she's been here three minutes,
and he's already on her."

Henry spoke before thinking. "You know her?"

"That yella-haired gal? Yeah." He looked at Henry and
grinned as his head swayed back and forth. "She's a good-
un."

"Uh-huh." It occurred to Henry that O'Leary might
have been keeping an eye out for the girl.

"The thing a man wants to do is catch 'em first off. That
Windsor, he's a bird dog, looks like." O'Leary looked back
around at Windsor and the saloon girl.

Henry nodded. The girl wasn't exactly wearing a hat of
ostrich plumes, but she did look pretty as a partridge. And
it gave him a small bit of pleasure to know that O'Leary
felt out-bird-dogged.

The next day, as Henry put in the gateposts for the corral
he had laid out, he couldn't get the episode with O'Leary
off his mind. On one hand, the invitation to meet in town
seemed to be a simple gesture of friendship, and the subse-
quent visit in the Gold Eagle had been sociable and
friendly. Henry had left before it was late, but O'Leary had
remained seated at the bar. On the other hand, it seemed
as if O'Leary might have been using him as an excuse for
going into town. O'Leary's envious remarks about Windsor, plus the comment about the yellow-haired gal, pointed
in that direction.

Then the whole idea of the bay horse came back. It was
a good-looking animal, not just an old plug of a plow
horse. From the impressions Henry had gathered on his
visit to Crow Creek, O'Leary wasn't set up well enough to

have forked out the cash—for that matter, he didn't even have much business quail hunting in town. Henry couldn't help laughing to himself. If O'Leary had paid Windsor even a portion of the price of that horse, it must have galled him to imagine Windsor spending the money on the saloon girl.

Then he told himself again that it was none of his business, which was a good way to put the thoughts aside when he had nearly worn them out anyway.

Henry took his time putting in the gateposts, eyeballing them from several different angles to try to keep them straight up as he tamped them in. He would not have the corral finished by the time he went to roundup, but he would have a good start. He had grown up hearing his father say that a job worth doing was worth doing well. Henry wanted a sturdy main corral, so he had paid good money to buy posts and planks that had been shipped in. Within a few miles he could cut a few cedar posts and enough cottonwood poles to build a fence or a holding pen, but for his main corral he wanted the best he could manage. He would not want to have to say about himself, as he had heard his father say about others, that a poor man had a poor way of doing things.

He looked at the dugout, which was a combination of rocks, cottonwood logs, and dirt. Now that was a different matter. It was just something to live in for the time being. When it came time to build a real house—when there was a woman in the picture—he would try to do his best there too.

Henry had laid out the corral at the base of the bluff next to the dugout, so he often had his back to the open country as he worked. When he heard Beau whiffle, he looked around at the picketed horse and then away to the east.

A horse and rider came toward them. This time Henry

recognized O'Leary and the bay horse immediately. From about a hundred yards out, O'Leary waved. Henry waved back.

The rider brought the horse in without any trouble this time, and as he dismounted he said, "Looks like I caught you workin' again."

"Yep. I thought I'd see how much I could get done on this corral before I went on roundup."

O'Leary nodded as he looked at the two upright posts. "Looks good so far."

"Well, thanks."

"Looks like you went all out and bought new."

"Just for the corral." He motioned with his head toward the dugout. "I can't afford to do everything first class at once."

"That's a good-lookin' little shanty," O'Leary said.

Henry wondered if the man remembered having said the same thing before, so he repeated what he himself had said on that same visit. "Well, it's a dugout, actually."

O'Leary gave no flicker of recognition. "Looks good to me. Still in good shape."

"It's not that old. I built it off and on in my free time last year. Then I spent a pretty good stretch of time in it this past winter."

O'Leary nodded, as if he wasn't really listening or as if his attention was wandering. Then he said, "Sure turned out to be a nice day, didn't it?"

"Sure did."

"Could even get warm."

"Uh-huh." Henry saw O'Leary glance at the shade that was just crawling out from the dugout. "Care to sit down for a while?"

O'Leary tipped his head to either side. "Oh, maybe for a few minutes. Long enough to let my horse cool down and then have him a drink."

"You can tie him up here." Henry pointed at the hitching rail and stood aside as O'Leary led the horse forward and stopped at the rail.

"I'll tell ya," said the red-haired man as he pushed his hat back, "this horse has to wait for his drink, but I'm about ready for one. And not just water. How about you?"

Henry looked at the sun and felt himself frown. "Might be a little early in the day."

"Just a little nip. I don't have enough here to do us any damage." O'Leary turned around to the bay horse, and with the reins still in his left hand he dug into the saddle-bag and drew out a pint flask wrapped in leather. He uncapped it and handed it to Henry. "Here's to bein' friends."

Henry took the flask and hesitated. Then he remembered a line he had heard one time from a sheepherder, a witty old graybeard named Manders, who liked to deliver polished lines. The sheepherder had said, "My door is open, and I drink from the cup that is offered to me." Henry smiled at the memory. Then he sniffed the open mouth of the flask, recognized the smell, and took a sip of whiskey. It burned all the way down his throat. He licked his lips, stretched his mouth tight, and handed the flask to its owner.

O'Leary tipped the flask in salute, then touched it to his lips and glugged what looked like a good-sized drink. He lowered the flask, winked his left eye, and tilted his head. Then he smacked his lips open. "Another?" he asked, handing the liquor back toward Henry.

"I'll wait."

O'Leary smiled. "It'll keep." He screwed the cap onto the metal neck of the flask and then wrapped his right thumb and forefinger around the cap and neck.

Leaving O'Leary to tie his horse, Henry went into the cabin and brought out two chairs. He set them in front of the doorway, beneath the deer antlers that were fixed to the cross beam. As they sat down, Henry noticed the flask in the other man's right hand. O'Leary must have caught the glance; he held the whiskey toward Henry, who shook his head. Then O'Leary uncapped the flask and tipped himself another swig.

After a long moment of silence, O'Leary spoke. "Was it a bad winter?"

Henry reflected. "No, not all that bad. Normal, I'd say."

O'Leary nodded and said nothing.

"Why do you ask?"

The visitor raised his eyebrows. "Seems to me there's a lot of orphan calves. Thought maybe there'd been some winter kill."

Henry thought back again. "Not so much, from what I've seen. Winter kill would get 'em both, either before the calf was born or before it could fend for itself. I think you'll see more cows without calves than the other way around."

"But you will see some mavericks."

"If you mean a calf that hasn't been branded, of course you will. Spring roundup is just starting." Henry paused. "I think you told me before that you'd come to this country just before I met you."

"That's right. I just been here a little while."

"Well, you know a calf gets branded according to the brand its mother carries."

The red-haired man pushed his hat back about an inch. "And those that don't have mothers, or aren't with one?"

Henry paused. "Used to be, the Association assumed all those. It's not quite that tight now, but it's not all wide open, either."

"But there are mavericks, and there'll still be some after roundup."

"Oh, naturally some get missed, but we catch most of them in the fall."

O'Leary smiled and rocked his head. "Seems to me

there's calves out there that a man could put his brand on."
He looked out around the country. "You could be workin'
on your own herd."

Henry's lips felt dry. He ran his tongue across them and
said, "I don't even have a brand yet. I put in for one but
haven't gotten it yet."

O'Leary set the flask next to the leg of his chair. "That
doesn't have to hold you back."

Henry looked at him and shook his head. He didn't like
the idea, but before he said much he needed to know for
sure what the other man was getting at. As he waited for
him to speak, he imagined O'Leary must have thought
there was more confidence between them than there was.

O'Leary went on. "I've got a brand. If you see a calf you
like, send him to me, or put my brand on 'im if you like.
Then I'll split with you."

Henry twisted his face but said nothing.

"It'll be just like I'm sellin' 'em to you. Give you transfer
papers and all. You can have the heifer calves and get your
own herd goin'."

Henry could see that the man was proposing an all-out
mavericking scheme with Henry as an inside man, but he
felt as if he hadn't caught up with the whole idea. "How are
you going to start your own herd with bull calves, then?"

"They'll be steers soon enough, and I got a place to send
'em. I got a market. All I need is a supply."

It was getting clear enough now. Henry looked at his
own boots and wished he hadn't gotten into the conversation. "Nah. It's not for me."

O'Leary picked up the flask and held it without opening
it. "What part of it doesn't look good to you?"

Without looking up, Henry said, "All of it."

"How?"

Henry looked straight at him. "Everyone knows that
calves come from somewhere. If you've got a small herd
and you bring in a maverick or two, that's normal. Just

about everyone does it, and it evens out all the way around. But if you show up with no cattle and all of a sudden you have a crop of calves to sell, it's pretty obvious."

"Those bull calves, or steers, they'll go out of the country pretty quiet, and the heifers could too, if you wanted. You'd get paid for the calves you supplied. Then you could buy your own stock from someone else."

Henry shook his head. "It's not for me. Just a few years back, a man couldn't ride for an outfit and keep his own place on the side, for just those reasons. Now there's a few, like Cyrus Blaine, that go along with the idea of a little man trying to get a start on his own, and I'm not about to make him wish he hadn't."

"You know best," O'Leary said.

Henry felt a sting in the remark. "Look," he said. "Even if I could get away with it, I wouldn't want to be known as someone who started his herd with the long rope." He looked straight at O'Leary again. "I just wouldn't want to do things that way."

The answer was quick. "No harm. No harm at all. It was just an idea, that's all. I see it as livin' off the land, and you see it a little different. I see it as just a business—the more you brand, the more you make. Not a lot different from furs or timber. You're a little more dug in here, and you see it different. No harm in that."

"I hope not."

"None at all. Propositions come and go everyday, and for as much as I know, this one might not go anywhere."

Henry nodded.

O'Leary laid the palm of his left hand flat on the top of the cap of the whiskey flask, then curled his fingers and thumb to loosen the cap. "Besides," he said, "there's better things to talk about."

As Henry exhaled, he felt as if he had been holding his breath. "I imagine," he said.

CHAPTER 3

BACK AT HIS work, Henry looked up every few minutes and watched O'Leary and the bay horse ride farther away. As the pair receded, they darkened and became one, until it was a dark speck in the distance. Then it disappeared in the grassy plain, like a flea on a dog's back.

Henry wondered how much the liquor had to do with O'Leary's proposition. He guessed that the newcomer had been working on the idea over a period of time as he made gestures of friendship. The maverick plan probably did not come from the bottle, but it might have come out when it did because of the liquor. O'Leary must have gotten a pretty good dose of the juice into his blood the night before and decided to chase it today. The hair of the hound, they called it.

Folks often said that liquor brought out the worst in a person; they also said it brought out the truth. Henry felt that in O'Leary he had seen more than a weakness for drink. O'Leary's remarks about the saloon girl, and then his proposed idea of how to live off the land, seemed to show the true markings of the man. Henry also knew that friends of long standing, especially if they drank together, tended to forgive or downplay the loose talk that came out with liquor. In this case, he would call O'Leary a friend of sorts because they had started that way, but he was not at a level of friendship or confidence that would let him overlook what had gone on.

He imagined that before long, O'Leary would realize he had overplayed his hand. Even though he had seemed to brush it away as a harmless topic that had merely lighted like a bug, he might wish he hadn't spoken so much so soon. Henry winced. He had been brought into a couple of different confidences he hadn't asked for, and now he was in a position where, from some other point of view, he might seem like a threat.

He shook his head. He didn't want any complications. In the last couple of years he had decided to try to give his life direction and not just live from one day to the next. He had come to see that trying to manage his life meant having to give up the carefree attitude of not caring about what came next. Life was serious enough now, with having to decide how to build his corral and plan the rest of his layout. He didn't need the added worry of wondering whether he should be looking over his shoulder.

Henry picked out a post that he thought would make a good corner post. He carried it to the hole he had just dug, set it in, and checked it for height. It was about an inch low, so he lifted it up and kicked in some dirt, rammed the post on the loose dirt a few times, and sighted across the top of the new post to the other two he had put in. Then he stopped and sighted them to see that they made a straight line. Everything looked fine, so he shoveled some dirt in around the post and began tamping. It was satisfying work, starting with a new plan and getting things in place, straight and solid.

The work made him feel good again, and he remembered how happy he had been the day before. He was almost that happy again, and despite O'Leary's intrusion, he still appreciated how good it felt to be alive. He glanced at the wild roses, bright with life, and then he looked at the neat stack of firewood he had piled the day before.

It had occurred to him that the firewood was dead, and dead things served the living. So was the post dead, this post that he held with one hand as he tamped with another. When he got it built, the corral would be strong and useful, and it should give long years of service. But he also knew that the simple things he built with his own hands—the corral, certainly the dugout, and the house if he built one—would someday be gone. It was his land, but it would be his for only a short while. Then he would go the way of the cedar tree, or that nameless tree that had lived and died on its own in the canyon.

The difference was that a man was free to move and act and try to shape his own life. Knowing that it was all for only a short stretch of time made him want to do the best while he could.

He worked on through the afternoon, and when he had all four corners as well as the gateposts tamped in solid, he called it a day. He put away his tools, tended to his horse, then built a little fire in the firepit. Even in the winter, a cooking fire sometimes heated up the dugout so much that he had to open the door, and when the weather was fair, it was far more pleasant to cook outside.

The dugout was a snug shelter, and mighty welcome in the winter. It had three sides of earth and the front side of peach-colored sandstone. The roof, resting on thick cottonwood ridge poles supported by stout uprights, consisted of a layer of slender cottonwood poles covered with a sheet of canvas and topped with the black-root sod he had dug out of the floor area. Inside, the dwelling measured twelve feet by fifteen and nearly eight feet high, which was plenty of room for one man, his tools, and his gear. But with no window it could be a gloomy place, and when the little rock fireplace didn't draw just right, it got smoky. All in all, though, he got good use out of it and expected to do so for a while to come.

After supper, which he cooked on coals of cedar wood, he burned some of the wood from that nameless tree in the canyon. The cool air came on with the night, and he enjoyed the fire for its warmth and company. After about an hour of darkness he let the fire burn down to gray coals, then went into the dugout to sleep.

In the morning he sat outside his door and sorted through his war bag. An ideal dugout was built into a south-facing bank, to catch the most benefit from the winter sun, but Henry's cabin, because of the natural distribution of the earth, necessarily faced east. The rock face of the cabin caught and held the warmth of the sun in the early part of the day, so that on a spring morning, it was a fine place to sit and drink coffee while he tended to small matters.

It looked as if he would run out of coffee before he went back to the ranch, and since he needed to buy a couple of little things to take with him on roundup, and since it was a Monday morning, he decided he would go into town. Before going, he checked through his personal effects and counted his money, which was easy to count after he had paid for the posts and planks.

The trip to town usually took two hours, so he saddled Beau and set out before the sun was very high. The day was just beginning to warm up by the time he got to town, and Beau did not seem heated up as Henry tied him to the hitch rack and loosened the cinch.

Inside the mercantile, he found two pairs of wool socks like the ones he was used to wearing. He had just picked them up when he was aware of another person coming near.

"May I help you find something?" It was a cheerful, female voice.

Henry looked up and around. He saw Molly Chardon, a young woman he had danced with at a couple of social events. She had dark eyes and long, dark hair. Her skin seemed to carry a light tan even through the winter.

"Well, hello," he said. "I didn't expect to see you here."

She smiled. "I work here now. Mr. Van der Linden offered me a job, so I came into town, took a room with the Sullivans, and went to work."

Henry glanced at her, trying not to look too long. He had a pleasing impression of a sky-blue dress, long at the sleeves but showing a little of the throat. "Your folks still live out on Sage Creek?" He had a quick image of the father, who was a trapper and a trader, and of her mother, who was dark-haired like Molly.

"Oh, yes."

"Doing well, I hope."

"Oh, yes. Everyone is fine."

"Your little sisters too?"

"Yes, growing like kittens."

Henry smiled, remembering the two girls. He knew that the Chardons had Indian blood on both sides of the family, and the little girls showed it. They were very pretty, giving promise that they would grow up to be attractive like Molly. He shifted the socks to his left hand, and as he did, he glanced again at the solid blue dress. Then he asked, "How long have you been in town?"

"Just about a month."

"You like it all right?"

"Well, I miss my family, of course. They haven't been to town since I came in, but I expect them to make it in one of these days. Otherwise—yes, I like it. It's new, and I've never lived in a town before, but, you know, I couldn't live at home forever. There just wasn't anything for me."

Henry nodded. On a farm or a ranch there was always plenty of work for anyone who was able, but the Chardons had just their cabin and a few head of horses. With the other two girls big enough to do chores and help around the house, it would make sense that Molly should go to town and have a job. Working girls usually helped the family, too. Henry looked her in the eyes and smiled, and as he did it he noticed a ribbon, sky blue like her dress, against the rich, dark hair. He imagined her little sisters would have ribbons now, and material for dresses. "Well," he said, "I hope everything goes well for you here in town."

"I'll get used to it," she said.

She raised her right hand to brush a stray hair from her cheek, and Henry admired the hand. It was slender and smooth, but not the delicate hand of a woman who had never worked. She lowered the hand and smoothed the dress against her hip. As she did so, she spoke. "And yourself? Are you still working for the Box Elder Ranch?"

He found himself meeting her eyes again. "I sure am. I'll be going back on roundup in a few days." Then, as an added thought, he said, "I have my own little place now, too, you know."

"Oh, really?"

"Out at Ruby Canyon. It's just a little quarter-section homestead, but it's something to give me a start."

"Ruby Canyon. Now, that's southwest of here, isn't it?"

"Yes, it is. That would be northeast of your place, or your folks' place."

She nodded in agreement.

"Southeast of the Box Elder," he added.

"Right."

Silence hung in the air for a second, as if the two of them were coming back to where they now stood. Then Molly spoke.

"Can I help you find anything else?"

Henry leaned his head to the right for a second. "Well, yes. I'd like a couple of little cakes of soap to take out on roundup, and half a pound of coffee beans to last me for the next few days before I leave."

"We've got both of those over by the counter," she said, and she turned around, swishing the light-blue dress.

Henry followed her to the counter and stood near her as she scooped the coffee beans, weighed them, and double-wrapped them in newspaper.

"Now for the soap," she said, moving around behind the

counter. "As for little bars, this is what we have." She held a small, pale, rectangular piece of soap toward him.

He took it in his hand and smelled it. It was nearly odorless. "That's fine," he said. "It's just that sometimes there's no soap when you want it, so I like to carry my own. Just in case." He handed it back to her.

"Two of them?"

"Please."

She set the two bars of soap on the counter and, pausing, said, "I imagine it would be better if I wrapped them separately."

Henry shrugged. "I suppose so. I won't use 'em both at once."

Molly reached under the counter and took out a sheet of brown wrapping paper, folded it, tore it in half, and wrapped each of the two pieces of soap. "There you are," she said, setting them next to his other purchases. "Anything else?"

"Not today," he answered.

"That will be a dollar and a half," she said.

He felt his face change as he reached into his pocket.

"It's the coffee," she said. "Mr. Van der Linden says he expects the price to come back down with the next shipment."

He looked at her and smiled. "Gotta have coffee."

She smiled back. "That's right." Then, accepting the money, she said, "Thank you, Henry."

"Thank you, Molly," he answered as he gathered up his items.

"Come again."

He looked at her and smiled. "I will. Now I know where to find you."

She smiled back. "Now you do."

Henry heard the tinkle of the bell as he closed the door behind him, and he paused on the sidewalk to try to remember if there was anything else he needed to do while he was in town. Then his attention went to his right, where he saw a man walking out of the bank.

It was Windsor, again in the light-colored hat. He was walking in the direction of the mercantile, so Henry just stood to let him go by. The man was looking straight ahead, with the air that self-assured, well-dressed men sometimes had—moving the head jauntily as he walked, pursing his lips as if whistling but not making any noise. Henry dropped his gaze to the board sidewalk and then moved it upward as the man came thumping along.

Windsor was a man who had apparently given some thought to his appearance. He wore gray boots, unlike the boots of most men Henry knew, as they were unscuffed. He wore a gray suit of lightweight wool, complete with vest, white shirt, and dark-gray cravat. A silver watch chain looped across the right side of the waistcoat, and a silver pin shone from the tie. Henry saw as before the silver Vandyke, the gray temples, and the reddish blond hair. He noticed that the eyes were blue-gray. Then he observed that the hat, which had a smooth, rounded ridge around the top of the crown, also had a narrow leather hatband with silver tokens or rivets on the front and sides. The tokens were round and about the size of the flat end of a .30-caliber cartridge.

Windsor walked by, paying no attention to the cowhand lounging in the doorway of the mercantile; as Henry got a back view, he saw a fourth silver ornament on the rear of the hatband. All the man needed was a cane to twirl, he thought.

Henry moved across the sidewalk and stepped down into the street. He looked around to catch another glimpse of Windsor, who was still walking down the sidewalk. Suddenly the dandy paused in midstride and looked over his shoulder, then moved on.

The maneuver sent a flicker of uneasiness through Henry. He was sure Windsor had not noticed him when he walked by, and there did not seem to be any other reason for the man to look back so suddenly. There was no unusual noise or movement to spook the man. The quick turnaround seemed to be automatic, unrelated to the present time and place. It was as if Henry had just seen two Windsors—one who was oblivious to his surroundings, and one who saw or heard things that weren't there.

He watched as Windsor came to the end of the block, crossed the street, and stepped back up to the sidewalk. Again the man gave a quick turn to the left, hardly pausing, and then moved on. Henry shrugged. The man was a dandy, and a strange one to boot. It would be hard to guess how he would fare in this country.

Henry put his purchases into his saddlebags, then led Beau down the street to water him before leaving town. When the horse had had a drink, Henry tightened the cinch, put his foot in the stirrup, and swung aboard. In a matter of minutes they were on the open plains, meeting a warm, light breeze from the southwest. The world seemed happy again, and the odd incident with Windsor seemed far away.

As he rode back to Ruby Canyon, Henry thought about seeing Molly at the mercantile. With pleasure he reviewed the image of her dark eyes, dark hair, tan skin, and blue dress. He also had an awareness of the packages he carried in his saddlebags—small and neatly wrapped by a pretty girl's hands. It would be a pleasure to carry those two bars of soap to roundup.

Back at the dugout, he saw the wild roses shining pink in the sunlight. He reminded himself that they had been blooming even when he wasn't there to see them. He looked from the pink roses to the blue sky above the bluff, thinking that the two colors went together very well.

CHAPTER 4

AS HENRY SAT in front of the sandstone face of the dugout in the cool of morning, he felt the urge to go to town again. Usually he did not care about town and did not miss it much in between his normal visits, but now he thought he'd like to go back. The thought of dark eyes, dark hair, and blue dress came to his mind over and over. He remembered her hands and the smooth tan of her face and throat.

He went through his war bag to see if there was something else he could imagine needing. As he had done the day before, he opened the drawstring of the light leather bag that held his sewing kit. He took out the small wooden case, opened it, saw again that he had enough needles, and closed it. Then he dumped the rest of the kit into his right palm—a spool of white thread and a little heap of assorted buttons. Maybe he could use another spool of thread.

As he put the kit away, he nodded. It seemed extravagant to ride all the way to town for a spool of thread, but it was as good an excuse as any and better than some. She would know, also, and there would be no harm in her knowing that he rode all that way just to see her again.

Henry looked at the unfinished corral. He would still get in some work on it today, and he didn't have a set date for finishing it anyway. He rubbed his cheek and thought that if he did go, he would shave first. He smiled and took a drink of coffee. His life was his own, and he had a little free time, which he wouldn't have again during the six weeks he would be on roundup. If he wanted to go to town, he could up and do it.

At about the same time as the day before, then, he saddled Beau and headed toward Willow Creek. The day came on warm and clear once again, and Beau moved at a fast walk. It gave a good feeling to be moving across the country at green-up time, with the birds singing and the prairie flowers blooming. The spring came back each year—not always exactly the same, but always spring, and always encouraging.

Although there was the illusion that time moved in a circle and always came back to the same point, Henry had seen enough years to know that the hoop or circle rolled forward. The birds and rabbits he saw now were just like the ones he had seen a year ago or five years ago, but when he thought about it, he knew they weren't the same ones. Even if one day seemed just like the day before, yesterday was gone and today had taken its place. Put a weld on the metal rim of a wagon wheel, and in soft dirt the weld would leave a mark farther along the trail each time it came around.

Henry took a deep breath and let it out. Life did go forward, whether a fellow recognized it or not. After a few years in Wyoming, he had begun to notice that many of the cowpunchers, and not just the new ones, were younger than he was. Some of these lads just coming onto the range had barely been born when he first went out on his own.

The eight years he had spent on the 6T6 Ranch in western Kansas were long gone—he could see that now. He had had a good horse and a good dog when he went to work on the 6T6, and when he left, they were both buried on the Kansas prairie. Life had seemed to stretch out new ahead of him when he rode Beau to Wyoming, just as it seemed to do now. But he knew he had crossed a couple of rivers he couldn't cross back. Some of life—even the newest part—was used up, and not all of life was yet to come. At thirty-three he was neither young nor old. He felt young, and he hoped life still had plenty to offer, but knowing that some of it was behind him made him realize that there were rivers ahead that he could cross only once.

Henry and Beau trotted into Willow Creek at about the same time as the day before. In front of one house, Henry saw a clump of blue flax shining in the morning sun. It was a rich blue, darker than the dress she had worn the day before, and he wondered if she had a dress that color.

Then the horse and rider were past that house and into the broad main street. Just as he had done the day before, Henry tied Beau at the hitch rack, stepped up onto the board sidewalk, and went into the mercantile. As the tinkling of the bell faded, he looked into a corner to adjust his eyes to the dim interior. As he looked up and around, he saw Molly standing in the aisle about twenty feet ahead of him.

She was smiling, and as he walked toward her she said, "Back so soon?"

"Couldn't stay away." He felt himself smiling.

She gave a short laugh. "You didn't use all that coffee already, did you?"

"No, nor the soap either."

She laughed again. "Something new, then?"

"Yes." He paused, his mind registering that the tan dress she was wearing was made of a fabric. On first view, in the distance and in the dimmer light, it had looked like tanned deerskin, which had not seemed out of place in the semiconscious way he had taken in the impression. Now as he corrected his own observation he noticed that the dress she wore today, like the one she had worn the day before, was of one solid color. The entire thought took only a second or two, and then he was looking her in the eye and saying, "Thread."

"Thread? For sewing?"

"Precisely," he said, and they both laughed.

Cupping her hands together in front of her, she asked, "What color?"

"I'd like a good, all-purpose color. For sewing on buttons, or mending a rip, or patching up a sock."

"Oh," she said, raising her eyebrows. "Then you didn't run out in the middle of a project, like some of the girls do, and come running in here for more."

Henry thought of his unfinished corral. "No, I don't have that kind of a project goin' on right now."

"More of an eye to the future, then."

He laughed. "That's right. I can count on having to sit out at least one rainstorm under a tent, and I can count on having something to mend by then."

"Well," she said, with the tease still in her voice, "most of the cowpunchers are stocking up on bright-colored threads this year—yellow and red and so on."

He winked. "I'd like something a little more serious."

"Well, let's see what we've got," she said, turning toward the counter.

Henry followed her and watched as she turned to the right in front of the counter and led them to a shelf against the wall. It was a part of the store he hadn't noticed before, and now he saw an assortment of sewing notions.

"You probably want something durable," she said, moving to her right to make room for him. Then before he could answer, she picked up a spool of black thread from the shelf and half-turned to show it to him. "This is good strong thread," she said. She opened her hand and let the spool rest in her palm.

He picked it up between thumb and forefinger and nodded.

"Here," she said, holding out her hand, "let me show you." She took the spool and pulled out a length of thread about a foot long. She wrapped the thread behind the lower fingers of each hand and gave a tug, then a visibly harder tug, and the thread snapped. She held the broken-off piece to Henry, who took it. Then she picked a spool of white thread from the shelf, unraveled a similar length, and gave it a small tug. It broke. She laid that piece in Henry's hand next to the first one. "You see? It really is stronger, and quite a bit thicker."

Henry nodded, looked at her, and smiled.

Her dark eyes were shining as she smiled back.

"I'll take it," he said.

"Anything else?"

He stepped back to let her walk by. "I don't think so. I'm pretty well fixed for needles."

"Think, now," she said, as she led the way back to the counter. "I wouldn't want you to get all the way home and then remember you were out of strychnine or bluing." She stepped behind the counter.

"I've got plenty of both," he said, "but if I ran out of either one, I'd come back in."

She set the spool on the counter and moved it toward him, and looking at him with the twinkle again in her eyes, she said, "That would be fine."

He handed her a silver dollar. As she looked into the cash drawer to make change, he said, "I probably won't be in for a while, though." He took a quick breath and said, "But when I get back from roundup, I'd sure like to drop by."

She held the change toward him, and he opened his hand to take it. Her hand barely touched his as she said, "That would be nice."

As their eyes met, Henry said, "Thank you, Molly."

"Thank you, Henry. And come again."

"I sure will." He pocketed his change and carried the spool of thread with him as he turned and walked to the door.

Out on the sidewalk, he was putting the thread in his vest pocket when he became aware of a person to his left, sitting on a bench up against the building in the shade. He turned and looked, and there was Van O'Leary smiling at him.

Henry felt a pang of uneasiness but tried not to show it. "Well, hello, Van."

"Howdy, Henry." After a short few seconds of silence, the man said, "I saw your horse here, and I was hopin' I might find you."

"Oh."

"But I didn't want to interrupt you while you were at business." O'Leary gave a closed-mouth smile. Then he said, "You wouldn't begrudge a man with red hair, would you?"

Henry glanced at the red hair, gave a quick laugh, and said, "No. Why?"

O'Leary laughed back. "Well, I've got a favor to ask of you."

Henry hesitated. O'Leary's joke was obviously calculated. "I guess it depends on what it is. You know, I've got to take off here in a few days, to ride with the wagon."

"This isn't much," said O'Leary. He stood up and gave Henry a level glance. "I've got to take off for a little while." He looked away and looked back. "Business trip. Be gone for a week or so."

"Uh-huh."

"And I was wonderin' if you might drop by my place once or twice while I was gone, to see if everything's all right." O'Leary looked out at the street and then back at Henry. "There's really not much to do, and Dora can make out all right. But she's worried about bein' left alone, and she trusts you. So if you could just drop by long enough to ask if everything's in shape, it would put her mind at ease."

Henry gave it a thought. O'Leary was giving him a chance to say no harm done. And it really wasn't much to be asking, since the wagon would roll in less than a week. If he declined, Mrs. O'Leary might think he was inconsiderate, and her husband might resent being snubbed. "I suppose I could," he said. "When do you leave?"

"Later today."

"Well, what would you think if I dropped by on the day after tomorrow? Then if there's anything that needs to be done, I can tend to it before I go away."

"I doubt you'll have to do anything more than just drop by and say hello."

Henry nodded. He had already imagined he would not go into the house, but if there happened to be a problem with the horse or the windmill, a helping hand would be welcome. "It should be no problem," he said. "You can tell her I'll be by the day after tomorrow."

"Thursday."

"That's right. And unless I hear otherwise, I expect to go back to the Box Elder on Saturday, the second."

"That's fine." O'Leary put out his hand, and as the two men shook, he said, "I appreciate it, Henry. I really do."

Over the next couple of days, as he worked on the corral, Henry thought from time to time about the spool of thread and the two neatly wrapped bars of soap in his ditty bag. More often, he thought of the girl who had touched them—a girl with graceful hands and a flashing smile, a girl named Molly who wore dresses of solid colors and worked in the store.

Less often, but still with some frequency, he thought of his obligation to O'Leary. He felt an uneasy friendship with the jovial man, something troublesome beneath the free-spirited exterior, but the requested favor was a reasonable one. If O'Leary had left on some questionable piece of business, that was his affair, and Henry was comfortable with being left uninformed of the details. In the meanwhile, at least on the surface, he could smooth out any wrinkles that might be left from the earlier confidence. It looked as if they could now pretend that the conversation about mavericks hadn't quite taken place—and if it had, that it was now in a haze.

By late afternoon on Thursday he had all of the corral

posts tamped in solid and even. Next he would have to measure, cut, and nail all the planks, which would be slow work for one man. He had a method figured out, though, and he imagined he would have most of the planks nailed on when it was time to go. At some point later on he would have to build and hang the gate.

The ride cross-country to the O'Leary place went briskly. With the sun at his back and the day cooling off, he gave Beau a loose rein. The horse had gotten well rested as he watched Henry dig holes and set posts, and now he moved out at a good pace. In less than an hour and a half, the O'Leary homestead came into view.

The place looked the same as it had on the earlier visit, and Henry could not see right away where O'Leary had done any new work. Henry rode into the yard and brought Beau to a stop in front of the house. He called out to see if anyone was home, and as the door opened he stepped down from the saddle.

Mrs. O'Leary closed the door behind her and came down the small wooden steps toward Henry. She stopped a couple of yards away and said, "Good afternoon."

Henry returned the greeting.

"Van said you might come by."

"He said he thought it would be a good idea, to see if you needed a hand at anything."

"I don't, really," she said.

In the moment's pause, Henry took a quick look at her. She had mouse-colored hair, somewhere between a blond and a brown, not very thick or wavy. It hung almost to her shoulders, and it framed a small, pale face. She had blue eyes, a small nose and mouth, and a small chin. In and around those features, she had a serious look on her face.

She spoke again. "It was nice of you to ride all the way over here. You really needn't have taken the bother. But Van probably thought I needed someone looking out for me."

Henry folded the loose ends of his reins with his left hand. "You never know. Something could come up. And you bein' new to the country, and all."

She gave a little smile. "There's not much to do, outside at least. We haven't gotten a garden worked up yet, and there's nothing but the horse to take care of. I've done a lot more than that on my own, before."

"Uh-huh."

"I mean it," she said. "I was raised in town, but I've learned how to milk a cow, feed hogs, dig potatoes." She raised her head. "When we lived in Ohio, he even used to have me flesh out his hides."

Henry sensed a tone of bitterness, although it was evident that her main purpose was to dismiss any worry about her helplessness. "Well," he said, "I imagine you're pretty able."

She gave the little smile again. "I suppose."

In the brief pause that followed, Henry's mind returned to a detail she had mentioned. "What kind of hides did he have you clean?"

"Fox, muskrat, coon—you name it. He trapped them all, and he loved to run his coon dogs."

Henry nodded. There was a glee he never understood in running dogs after raccoons. Shooting critters to protect a man's interests made sense, and trapping furs did, too. But running the animals just for the chase and kill was foreign to him.

Silence held for another few seconds, and he took a broader glance at her. She had a small build, neither shapely nor heavy, and her hands had obviously seen the type of work she had mentioned. But she was clean, which was not always the case among nester folks.

Henry took a deliberate breath and said, "Well, I'm glad to see that everything's all right."

She looked down and then up at him. "Everything's fine. And I certainly appreciate the trouble you went to."

"No trouble at all." Henry shifted his weight, thinking of what he might say next to put him on his way.

She spoke. "Can I offer you something? Some coffee? I would hate to have you ride all the way over here and then turn around and go home without at least offering you a cup of coffee. Or a drink of water, or something."

Henry considered. "A glass of water would be as good as anything." He nodded toward Beau. "And I imagine my horse would like a drink, too."

Mrs. O'Leary smiled, a little more broadly this time. "I believe you've watered him here before. If you'd like to do that, I'll bring out some water for us."

When Henry had finished letting the horse drink, he saw that Mrs. O'Leary had set out two chairs on the shady east side of the house. In front of the chairs on a wooden crate sat a tray with two tumblers and a pitcher of water. Henry tied Beau to the hitching rail in front of the house, and as he moved to take a chair, Mrs. O'Leary poured two glasses of water.

"Thank you, ma'am," he said, taking the glass she handed him.

"Please call me Dora."

"All right. Thank you, Dora."

"You're welcome. We were on a first-name basis when you came to dinner, you remember."

"Yes, we were." Henry took a drink of water. It was not cold but it was not tepid, either.

"Van said you'll be going off on a cattle roundup."

"That's right. In a couple of days. As I might have mentioned before, I ride for the Box Elder outfit."

"Yes."

"Over north and west of where I have my little place."

"It's a lot of hard work, isn't it?"

"Oh, sure. But it's what I do. I'm used to it." Henry looked at the glass in his hand.

"Mr. Sommers."

He looked at her, wondering why she didn't use his first name. "Yes?"

"I don't know you very well, but I feel that I have to tell you something."

Henry raised his eyebrows. When he looked at her face he thought he saw a pleading look. "Go ahead," he said.

"I hope you don't become too good a friend with Van."

Henry put the glass on his knee and held it there. For all that it seemed like good advice, he didn't like hearing it from the man's wife. Drawing his brows together, he said, "I don't know how much is too much, or too good, but I don't know him all that well to begin with. I don't see that much of him, and for the next six weeks at least, I'll be seeing even less."

Her face still had a troubled look as she answered. "It would be just as well."

"I appreciate your warning, Mrs. O'Leary. But I didn't just fall off the turnip wagon." As soon as he said it, he realized he might have been too blunt.

She looked down. "I just felt I had to say something. I know him better than you do."

Henry tried to sound agreeable. "No doubt you do."

"Well, all I meant is you may think you know him, but take my word for it—he keeps a lot to himself."

"I would imagine. But I look out for my own self, too. I've been paddling my own canoe for quite a while." He drew his lips back in a straight smile.

She gave a half-smile in return.

Henry drank the rest of the water and handed her the glass. "Thank you," he said, rising from the chair.

She set the two glasses on the tray and stood up with him. "Thank you for coming. I hope I didn't make you feel uncomfortable."

"It's all right."

She held out her hand. "Maybe I needed to say it as much as I thought you needed the advice."

He shook her hand lightly. "Think nothing of it." He walked to the horse and gathered the reins, then moved to the left side to mount up. He slapped a fat mosquito on Beau's neck, wiped his hand on the saddle blanket, and looked across the horse toward the woman. He touched the brim of his hat and said, "Good luck, Dora."

"The same to you, Henry."

He swung into the saddle, reined around, and waved. She waved back. A hundred and fifty yards out, he looked back and saw her still standing in front of the little homestead. He waved again, and the woman, looking smaller and sadder as she stood alone on the prairie, waved back.

CHAPTER 5

THERE WAS NO way to feel good about it. The picture of the woman stayed with Henry all the next morning as he cut and nailed planks on the corral. He felt sorry for her, but there was nothing he could do. A man didn't butt into someone else's affairs just because a woman was miserable. What O'Leary probably needed was a good thrashing, but he probably wouldn't get one, and even if he did, there would be no guarantee that life would improve for his wife.

It was hard to tell whose idea it had been to have him drop by. Each of them had made it seem like the other's idea. Either way, she had seen an opening and had taken it. Henry couldn't blame her for speaking up as she had done, since she was acting in his interest, but he wished he hadn't been drawn in to that point. He had thought he might be easing out by doing O'Leary a favor, but now he felt squeezed on both sides.

He was certain of one thing, though. He would try to have little to do with either Van or Dora. Six weeks on the range would help. And if he knew his man at all, which he thought he did to some extent, O'Leary wouldn't stay long in this country. Even the hardest-working homesteaders had a tough go of it, and someone like O'Leary, who thought he could make it on his cleverness, would likely foul his nest before too long.

Henry had finished his midday dinner and rest and had gone back to his work when he saw a visitor riding in from the northeast. As the rider came in closer, Henry identified him as Willis Finch.

Henry set down his hammer and walked away from his

work to meet the visitor. Finch, a fellow cowpuncher at the Box Elder, was riding one of the ranch horses from his string. It was a large, solid-brown gelding that was fit to carry a blocky man like Finch across the country.

Finch wore a brown hat with a pinched crown and a round, flat brim. His face, clean-shaven as always, was in shade as he brought the horse to a stop and looked down at Henry. "Stayin' busy?"

"I manage. How about you?"

"Some." Finch swung down, ran the first three fingers of his right hand inside the horse's cinch, and tied the reins to the hitching rail. He pushed back his hat, and Henry saw the familiar blue eyes beneath the dark eyebrows that almost touched. The eyes were always looking, and now they went to the corral and back to Henry. "Looks like your corral is comin' along."

Henry glanced at it. "Little by little."

"Don't let me keep you from it. I just stopped in for a few minutes—and, hell, while I'm at it, I'll help you put up a few boards."

"Might as well," Henry said. He and Finch were not close friends, but they had worked together plenty. Henry led the way to the corral, showed Finch what he was up to, and soon had a helper to hold up the other end of the plank. Henry imagined Finch had dropped by to remind him about the upcoming ranch work, but since the other man seemed in no hurry to state his business, Henry was in no hurry to ask.

They worked together for nearly an hour and finished the second rail up from the ground. Henry had worked all morning to nail on the bottom row and part of the second one, but with two men, the work went about three times as fast. When they finished the second band, Finch stood and rested with his hand on the gatepost.

"Gonna put a cap on it all the way around?"

"If I have enough lumber. It'll be pretty close."

"I'd have put the cap on first, brought the top rail snug up to it, and worked my way down."

Henry shrugged. "That wouldn't be bad, if I was sure I had enough lumber. Maybe I'll do it that way next time."

Finch looked at him with the blue eyes. "Are you gonna build another one?"

Henry laughed. "Not for a while."

Finch took a folded handkerchief from his hip pocket and wiped his brow. Then he looked at the sun. "I should probably head back. The boss said that if I saw you I should remind you to show up tomorrow."

"I was planning on it."

Finch nodded and put the handkerchief away. He untied the brown horse and led him to the trough to drink.

Henry stood by and watched. Finch always had a confident air about him, and even though he was three or four years younger than Henry, he acted as if he had greater wisdom. He was known for being good at handling horses, and Henry imagined he might have gotten some of his self-assurance through knowing he had that reputation.

"Lotta work," Finch said over his shoulder.

Henry assumed he meant the roundup. "I'd say so."

Neither man spoke until Finch backed the horse away from the water trough. Then the blue eyes flickered at Henry.

"I almost forgot."

"Oh?"

Finch reached inside his vest, a lightweight leather vest that he always kept buttoned. Because of his build, it fit him fairly snug, so reaching inside was the work of two fingers. He brought out an envelope and extended it to Henry. "For you."

Henry did not recognize the handwriting, and there was no postage on the envelope. He looked a question at Finch.

"Personal delivery." Finch gave a half-smile, and then he was on the big horse and trotting out of the yard, calling out "So long" over his shoulder.

Henry broke open the envelope, took out the letter, and unfolded it. Glancing at the bottom, he saw who had written it.

Henry—

I feel troubled about our visit. I'm afraid I've told you both too little and too much. Now I feel that I need to clarify, and I fear that you'll go off to the cattle roundup and leave things pending for six or eight weeks.

If you have time to ride over, it would be a great favor. If not, I will remain

Your friend,
Dora

Henry read the letter a second time and then folded it and put it back in the envelope. He had hoped to put this little entanglement at a distance, and here it had come back to him already, through the unlikely hands of Willis Finch. The letter promised some sort of resolution or tidying up. Dora probably wanted to tell Henry something he already knew, which meant that he would ride over there and back for the purpose of putting her mind at ease. Then again, there was no guarantee it would be that simple.

He disliked the problem coming back so soon, but as he thought about it he recalled how sad she seemed, a woman having to live out her troubles in isolation. He decided it was the least he could do—ride over, let her have her say, and be done with it.

The trip to the homestead on Crow Creek had the outward signs of the trip from the day before. The sky was blue, the grass was green, and the low-lying carpet flowers were white and yellow. Within him, though, apprehension weighed more heavily. He did not think that he could have snubbed her and felt justified, so he did what he thought he had to do—hoping the little intrigue would unwind itself, and dreading it might not.

He rode into the yard and called at the door, and she appeared, wearing the same print dress of faded blue and green. Henry dismounted, and as he tied Beau to the hitching rail he said, "I got your letter."

"I'm sorry," she said.

"For what?" He thought she might mean the manner in which she sent the letter.

"For putting you to this trouble."

"It's all right." He paused and then said, "I was a little surprised, though, at the way it came to me."

"Oh."

"Is he a friend of your husband's?"

"No, but I think he'd like to be a friend of mine. He heard Van was out of town—or away, I guess—and he came to see if I needed a hand at anything." She laughed. "So I asked him to carry a letter."

Henry laughed. He imagined O'Leary would not have appreciated Finch's visit, which probably fell in the category of bird-dogging, and he saw some humor in the wife's maneuver. He looked at the ground and then up at her. "Well," he said, "if you'd like to bring out the chairs, I suppose I could hear the rest of your story."

Mrs. O'Leary set up the chairs and the water pitcher while Henry watered Beau, and then he was seated again in the shade of the little house.

The woman took a deep breath and, with a manner that suggested she had thought out what she was going to say, began. "I don't imagine my husband has told you very much about his married life."

Henry shook his head. He had been expecting some indirect question about calves, cattle, or ranching, so the topic took him by surprise. "No, not really."

"I told you yesterday that he keeps things hidden."

"I think you said he kept a lot to himself."

"Yes. Well, he does." She paused. "I don't suppose he has told you he was married before."

"No, he hasn't ever mentioned it."

"I didn't know it until after we came here."

Henry widened his eyebrows but said nothing. He could tell she was determined to use the occasion and not waste any time.

"You look as if you want to say something," she said.

"Well, it seems a little odd, all right, if he hadn't ever mentioned it before."

"He had a good reason."

"Oh?"

"That other marriage never came to an end."

"You mean he's—"

"—a bigamist. Yes, that's what I mean. I found some papers while I was rearranging things shortly after we moved in."

Henry let out a long breath. "And you've been married—what, two years? I think that's what you said when I visited before."

"A little over two years now."

Henry shook his head slowly. "I guess I don't understand it. Of course, all I know is what you just told me." He looked at Dora. "Does he know you know?"

"Oh, yes. I confronted him."

"Did he give you any idea why?"

"He made it seem like it had been an ordeal, and one day he just walked away."

"Where did this all happen?"

"In Kentucky. That's where he's from." She looked across at Henry.

"I thought he was from southern Ohio."

"I am. I'm from Cincinnati, which is on the border. He

was living in southern Ohio when we met, and we lived there after we were married."

"That's where you learned to milk a cow, then."

"Yes."

Henry looked at his water glass. "Well, that's quite a surprise. And the other—wife—she still lives there? In Kentucky?"

"As nearly as I know."

Henry remembered O'Leary's comment: *If I had a son today, I'd name him Grover.* Maybe he was lying—he might already have a son or daughter. "It still doesn't make sense," he said. "I know men run off on their wives, but why would he turn right around and get married again?"

Dora gave him a steady look. "I don't know for sure. But I think he needs someone to put the blame on."

"Blame for what?"

"For everything, whatever upsets him." She sniffed, rubbed her finger across her nose, and looked back at the ground. "Sometimes I get so angry that I don't want to have anything to do with him. Then he goes on about what a poor wife I am, and he has things his way, then we're back where we started." She looked up. "Sometimes I feel like I'm in prison."

Henry felt an uneasy feeling in his stomach. "Have you thought about doing anything about it? I would imagine there's something you could do. I don't know what."

She was looking at her hands. "I'm still thinking it through." She looked up at him. "But you're right. I don't have to live like this. I come from a decent family—not rich, but there's nothing wrong with us." She shook her head. "I just need a plan."

He felt the queasiness in his stomach. "Does all of this that you're telling me today—does this have anything to do with what you told me yesterday, about hoping I didn't become too good a friend of his?"

She drew her head back. "Oh, no. I meant something else. I think you followed it. I meant his business deals."

"That's the way I took it." Henry let his breath out.

"But I felt that I needed to tell you the rest of it, so you would know how much he can't be trusted."

Henry opened his eyes wide. "I guess." He knew in that moment that all he had was her say-so, but from her tone and presence, he believed her. It did not seem likely that she would make up such a story, which she obviously saw as a discredit to herself. "I can see where you're stuck," he said. Henry took a drink of water.

She had a pained look on her face. "I just don't have a plan yet. I need to get things in the right order. I'm a long way from home. I tried to leave once, at the beginning when I first found out."

"And no luck?"

"No. He stopped me. That's why I need to think things out, or he'll just break me down every time."

Henry let out another long breath. "I don't know what I could do, even if you asked."

She looked at him. "I'm not asking anything right now—except that you listen, I guess."

"You just wanted to tell me—and that's more or less it?"

"I wanted you to know. So that if I did something, you wouldn't think bad of me."

He set his glass on the tray. "Ma'am—or Dora—if you caught the next train out of this country, I wouldn't blame you in the least. Quite the opposite."

She smiled. "That's as much as I could ask." She set her glass on the tray next to his. "And I appreciate your taking the trouble to come over again. I know you're running out of free time, and I feel rather selfish for asking you to come over, but—"

"It's all right." He gave what he thought was a reassuring smile, then stood up.

She stood up as well, moving half a step toward him as she offered him her hand.

He gave her hand a light shake and released it. Then he put his hand on her shoulder and nodded assurance, and as he did so, she moved toward him and laid her head on his chest. He patted the back of her head, feeling a motion within him but not acting on it. "You'll be all right," he said.

She looked up at him. The pale blue eyes were moist. "Thank you," she said.

He and she parted, and the unexpected motion he had felt was subsiding. He walked to his horse, untied him, turned him around, and climbed on. He touched his hat brim and said, "Good luck, Dora."

"Thank you, Henry. And the same to you."

At a little ways out he turned and waved, and she waved back. It didn't seem as sad as the day before, but as he rode on, he began to absorb the entirety of the conversation. It had ended on a positive note, so that the sight of the woman standing alone did not seem terribly mournful, but overall it was a sorry mess to know about—especially since he had been drawn in on both sides.

He gave deliberate thought to what might be her purpose in reaching out to him, and he concluded that she didn't have a definite purpose. As she had said, she didn't have a plan, and she had just needed someone to talk to. Henry thought about the physical movement she had made toward him, and he did not see it as anything overt. He interpreted Dora's actions as an indication she was uncertain, unsure of herself. Being that way had probably helped bring her and Van together, and judging from her story, Henry imagined Van had helped her stay that way.

He might have done Dora some good by hearing her out, but he hadn't done himself any. Now he knew even more about O'Leary, more that he wished he didn't know, and even though he hadn't asked to know any of it, the sensation crept into him that he was at fault for learning it.

Coming up out of a swale, he saw two horses and one rider coming toward him from the southwest. Beau gave a whiffle, and Henry turned him to meet the path of the other rider. There was no need to seem to be on the dodge.

As the other horses came nearer, Henry saw that the rider was the strange newcomer, Windsor. He wore a light-colored hat and neat clothing, and he was leading the bay horse of O'Leary's.

Henry's first thought was that something might have happened to O'Leary, but the horse carried no saddle. Henry continued to ponder as he came up to the group. "Hello," he said.

"Good afternoon," said the other man, with a grave tone to his voice. "Do we know each other?"

"I don't believe we've met. I'm Henry Sommers."

The other man touched his hat with his left hand and kept the right one lowered from sight, making no movement to shake hands. "I'm Gerard Windsor. I'm on my way to the O'Leary place." He looked sharply at Henry. "You're a friend of his, aren't you?"

"Um, yes. I'm just coming from there."

"I take it Mrs. O'Leary is at home."

"Yes, she is." Henry paused. "Her husband went on a trip, and he asked me to drop in and check on things."

"Good idea on his part." Windsor raised the lead rope with his right hand. "This is a horse of his. I sold it to him a little while back, and it decided to come back to my place. I knew Van was away, but I thought Mrs. O'Leary might like to have it back, so I'm delivering it."

Henry nodded. "Well, I'm sure she's still at home."

"Good enough. She's not expecting me, but I'm sure she'll be glad to see the horse."

"I'm sure."

"Good enough. Well, I won't keep you, and I should be moving on myself if I hope to be home by dark."

"Yes, sir." Henry touched his hat. "It's been a pleasure to meet you."

"All mine." Windsor touched his hat, nudged his horse, and moved away.

Henry put his heels to Beau and headed back in his original direction toward Ruby Canyon. After he had gone a little ways, he stopped and turned the horse so he could see Windsor. There was a chance that the other man would turn and see him watching, but he made himself take that chance. As it turned out, Windsor continued riding straight ahead without so much as shifting in the saddle. In the brief encounter a few minutes earlier, he had seemed austere and in possession of himself, and now as the man rode out of view, Henry decided that it was the self-assured Windsor and not the edgy one who still sat in the saddle.

Henry put Beau in the direction of home again, and with his back to Windsor, he thought about some of the other details. That bay horse was always good for a surprise. Now, why would O'Leary have gotten himself a new riding horse and then ridden away on his old one, which was supposed to be Dora's horse? The answer came right after the question. Dora would be less likely to go anywhere if she had an unfamiliar horse—and if she knew someone was going to check on her. Henry shook his head. O'Leary had a lot of moves.

Henry thought back again to consider what might have been O'Leary's motive in asking him to check in on his wife in the first place. It seemed as if it was an open show of confidence—almost a challenge—calculated to make Henry feel it would be a betrayal of confidence if he publicized the maverick proposition. O'Leary's motive might have been simpler than that, but whatever it was, Henry was sure the outcome was not what his neighbor intended. O'Leary must have been confident his wife wouldn't spill the beans, and she had done just that.

Henry could feel the uneasiness spreading in his stomach. He realized that despite his own efforts, it was as if he had violated that trust—not in the way Finch might have liked to, but by listening to Dora's story. His sharing the knowledge was an act of intimacy, and his possession of the knowledge now amounted to a secret between himself and another man's wife—a man who, on the surface, was a friend. Henry shook his head. While he had been talking with Dora he had felt sympathetic, but now he was glad he hadn't gotten in any deeper by offering to help. No, he thought, he needed to ease out if he could. He looked across his horse's ears, and he had one idea. If there was a way out of this, it was not to act on anything he knew about O'Leary—and to stay clear of both of them if he could.

CHAPTER 6

THE NEXT MORNING found Henry up early, putting his dugout in order. He set the coffee and sugar up with the flour, rice, and beans, all of which he kept on a shelf suspended by wire from the cottonwood rafters. He hadn't had much trouble with mice, but he knew that leaving a place on its own for a while was an open invitation for the rodents to move in. For that same reason he rolled up his bed, tied it with twine, and hung it from a ridgepole. A heavy cotton sack holding winter clothes was similarly rolled and tied to the ceiling, and in back of it hung a long bundle of burlap. Inside that bundle, he kept his rifle stashed.

He looked around the inside of the cabin and nodded, satisfied that everything was in order. In his mind he saw his war bag, which held the thread and the two bars of soap, already wrapped in his slicker and tied to the back of his saddle. He blew out the lantern and closed the door.

Henry saddled his horse as the first pink skies of morning began to show in the east. He could see the corral and the woodpile as the gray light spread, and a few seconds later he was able to make out the rosebushes against the bank. The roses would bloom on in his absence, smiling beneath the open sky as the meadowlarks sang and the sun crossed over.

Henry walked Beau out for a few yards, checked the cinch, and climbed on. He took a last look around and nudged Beau into movement. Then in the still of early morning he heard the creak of saddle leather and the clip-clop of hooves as he rode away.

* * *

Henry could hear men's voices as he neared the Box Elder headquarters. He knew that some men would be working with the horses while others would be getting the chuck wagon and the bed wagon ready to roll. The whole outfit would move out in two more days. Henry could feel it in the air—the energy of men and horses with springtime in their blood. The season was really under way again, for the cycle of a cowpuncher's work began with this, the spring roundup.

The Box Elder took part in an organized campaign called a pool roundup. Cyrus Blaine's outfit would put in with two other outfits—the Delmore and the 7-Bar—and between them they would cover the open range that lay in the vicinity of those three ranches. As the crew moved across the country and closer to the territory of other ranches, those outfits would each send a representative. As reps came and went, the total number of riders would vary from fifteen to twenty. In addition, there would be the roundup boss, Cyrus Blaine; a night wrangler and a day wrangler, supplied by the other two ranches; and the Box Elder cook, Hollis. Cyrus would provide the chuck wagon and the bed wagon, as in years past. The other two outfits, which were not set up quite as well as the Box Elder, would make up the deficit by hiring an extra rider each and fitting him out with a string of horses.

When the spring roundup was over, most of the men would stay on with the same outfit for summer work. As the open range gave way here and there to fenced farms and pastures, the work on a cattle ranch was shifting. There was more haying, especially after the bad winter of '86–87, which still loomed big in the memory of cattle country. A ranch always had barn and corral work, and now there was more and more fence work as well, and some ranches had ditches to clean. The summer work would keep the men busy until September or early October, when they would go back to long days in the saddle during fall roundup. The end of the cycle would come when they drove this year's beef to the railroad to be shipped to Eastern markets.

Henry unsaddled Beau and turned him out in the pasture. From now on it would be company horses, the good with the bad. Henry left his bag on his cot in the bunkhouse, then took his rope to the big corral, where the men had brought in the horse herd. He already knew the seven horses that would make up his string, and he planned to ride each one at least twice before the crew set out.

Finch was leading a big white horse out of the corral, so Henry held the gate. Finch darted a look his way and said, "You made it."

"Oh, yeah."

"Well, they're full of sap." Finch gave the lead rope a tug and walked away with the white horse.

Henry moved inside the corral and closed the gate behind him. Not far away, at the edge of the crowd of horses, stood a blue roan from Henry's string. "Hey, Dobber," he called, holding the coils of his rope close to his leg. In another minute he had a horse on the end of his line, and the day's work was under way.

He had ridden three horses without any trouble by the time the sun was straight up. His fourth horse was a deep-chested sorrel named Jake, who humped his back when the saddle went on. Henry remembered the horse well. Jake had stepped on Henry's foot once, and only once. Jake also had the habit of kicking at flies on his belly, a habit that he sometimes converted into a kick at a man, and Henry was determined not to let the old boy get at him that way. He kept Jake snubbed close, and he worked carefully around him as he settled the saddle onto him and reached under him to draw the cinch. He pulled the latigo through the cinch ring and was snugging it when he heard the dinner bell. That was just fine, he thought. The saddle was tight enough that it wouldn't slip to either side, and the horse was tied short enough that he couldn't do himself any damage. It would do him good to have to stand and stay put for a while.

The ranch hands had no hurry as they took their dinner, for everyone knew that it would be eat and run when they got to the range. They would take their time while they could. Even so, the bunkhouse manner was to eat first and talk later.

As he was working his way through the potatoes, gravy, and fried steak, Henry noticed a youngster helping serve up the grub. Earlier in the morning he had seen the kid stocking supplies in the chuck wagon. Now he got a better look. The kid was tall and spindly, with bony shoulders. He had long blond hair tucked behind his ears, and his chin jutted forward.

Henry looked at Finch, who was sitting across the table. "Who's the kid?"

Finch looked up and around. "That young willowtail? Why, that's Fred."

Henry looked at the back of the kid's head as he walked into the kitchen. The youngster did bear some resemblance to a broom-tailed horse. "Cook's helper?"

"Wants to be a cowpuncher. Talked the boss into givin' him a job."

"Is he going to go with the wagon?"

"Uh-huh. Cyrus the soft touch. Made an extra job for the kid, so he could learn to wrangle horses and maybe work his way up in another ten years."

Henry went back to his plate and said nothing. He knew Finch was proud of having broken right in as a regular hand when he was eighteen, and he could sense some resentment on Finch's part.

As the kid came back into the mess room with a plate of biscuits, Finch glanced at him and then said to Henry, "Of course, maybe he'll make a top hand."

Henry almost laughed. He thought it was generous of Cyrus to give the kid a break, but Fred didn't look like the type that would end up with his own string of horses.

After dinner, the men retired to the part of the bunkhouse that held their living quarters. There they stretched out to take a midday rest, and those who smoked could take their leisure that way.

Andy Galena sat in a chair by the open doorway and smoked his cigarette. He had a habit of chewing on the twisted end of a smoke after he had rolled and lit it, so he sat by the doorway where he could spit out the flecks of tobacco. He also had a habit of swatting flies with a buggy whip, so he kept the whip in one hand and the cigarette in the other.

Finch, who did not smoke, lay with his hands clasped behind his head of dark brown hair. "You know," he said, "back home we have flies in the winter, and folks that get shut in for the winter, they take to swattin' flies. I knew one fella took it so seriously that when spring came and there was a good hatch of flies at the stockyards, he took to goin' after them outside too."

"Don't worry about me," said Andy. He was about the same age as Finch, but he looked older. He had a ridge of brown curly hair, and above that rose a white, bald dome that never saw the sun. He had light brown eyes, a round nose and round lips, and a pair of ears that stuck out from the head enough to be noticed. He had a soft-looking build, but Henry knew better. Andy was as strong as any man on the place, and he was a good all-around worker with animals and tools. Handy at iron work, he kept the sickle bars and hay rakes going all through the haying season. He and Finch and Hollis, the cook, were the only ones who were kept on winter pay, and he didn't ever seem to let Finch's remarks get under his skin. Now he put the cigarette in his mouth and swatted a fly on the wall next to the stovepipe. The fly landed by the doorway, so he flicked it outside. "Don't worry about me," he said again. "I'll just get the ones that come to me."

Charlie Dan Logan, who also smoked, sat up on his bunk and rolled a cigarette. He would smoke in the bunkhouse, or around the campfire, and in town, of course, but as a habit he did not smoke on horseback or otherwise out on the range. Henry appreciated how Charlie Dan did things so neatly. He jiggled the Bull Durham sack with his little finger and spread tobacco into the trough of paper. Then he rolled a tight smoke, quirled the ends, and popped a match. "Kill one fly, kill a million," he said.

"That's right," Andy said. "A dead one will breed no more."

The talk went on that way for a little while, and at about the time that Henry thought about going back out to work with Jake, the willowtail kid came into the room and sat down on a bunk. He reached underneath the bed and brought out a pipe and a pouch, and with some show he loaded and lit the pipe.

It must have been too much for Finch, who spoke up. "I could give you a little tip on how to manage that pipe, kid."

Fred puffed out a big cloud, moved the stem to the corner of his mouth, and said, "Sure. Go ahead."

"Next time you go to the outhouse, toss it down the hole. Unlit. And if you still think you need to smoke one, get yourself one with a curved stem."

"Why's that?"

"A straight stem has got your pipe out there where it'll bump into any close work you're doin', or it'll catch a tree limb. And if your horse throws his head up, he can jam that stem down your throat."

The kid took the pipe out of his mouth and then put it back in.

"Just a little tip," Finch added.

"I appreciate it."

Finch sat up and swung his feet onto the floor. "Well, I suppose it's time to get back to work."

The others agreed, and within a couple of minutes they were all out in the sunlight, leaving Fred to sit alone and smoke his pipe. Henry felt sorry for the kid, but it was time to go back to work. And, he thought, part of making the grade was learning how to take the kind of nettling that Finch put out.

Henry worked through the afternoon, arriving at an understanding with Jake and then making his way through the other three horses in his string. The shadows were starting to reach out across the ranch yard when he turned the last horse into the corral and went to help Charlie Dan pitch hay.

At suppertime the men put on another good feed, and one by one they put their plates and utensils in the dishpan and went into the next room to relax. The small talk went on as usual until Fred joined the group, and then the atmosphere seemed to change. The men had been talking about cattle and ranching, and now Finch brought the subject around to crooked outfits. Finch was from Missouri and spoke with a faint accent that sometimes grew more noticeable when he said certain things.

"I'll tell you wot," he said. "You won't always know a crooked outfit when you see one. It might look like an honest setup, and they'll take on a few new hands, usually young fellers, that are good with a gun and a rope. They'll let these new hands buy into the outfit, and then if the operation gets uncovered, the ring-leaders slide on out and leave these youngsters in it up to their necks."

Fred did not seem to pay any special attention but rather focused on stuffing and lighting his pipe.

"Young feller from down by my hometown, down near Saint Joe, he got took up by one of them outfits, and now he's down in the state pen in Rawlins, learnin' to braid horsehair halters and cinches."

Henry looked at Fred, who still seemed to be giving Finch the brush-off.

The talk changed from that topic to another, and before long they were talking about the changes in the country. They all recognized that the open range was on its way out, what with more and more homesteaders taking up claims, fencing off streams and waterholes, and tearing up the range land. Few cowpunchers liked it, but there was no argument against a person's right to homestead.

"Lots of regular hands take up land," said Charlie Dan.

Andy spoke up. "And then turn it over to the company."

"Some don't," Charlie Dan answered. "Like Henry here. They just want something they can call their own. Isn't that right, Henry?"

"I guess."

"And there's plenty of them that give up and sell out," said Finch. "Henry's friend O'Leary got his from a quitter, and he's not doin' much better with it himself. I bet that place changes hands three or four times before it ends up part of some big land-and-cattle outfit."

Charlie Dan looked at Henry. "Is he a friend of yours?"

"In a manner of speaking."

Finch spoke up. "O'Leary's little woman said they were friends. Such good friends that Henry went over there two nights in a row."

Henry could feel his temper rising. "O'Leary said he was going to be gone for a while, and he asked me to drop by and check on things. Is there anything the matter with that?" He looked at Finch, who just shook his head. Then Henry went on. "And besides, I wasn't the only one to drop in." He could see Finch tensing up, and then he had his moment. "The good neighbor Windsor made a visit, too, to bring back a stray horse." Finch's face went blank, showing no expression.

Andy pushed a toothpick against his lower lip. "Windsor's the new money that came in, isn't he?"

Charlie Dan said, "That's right. And if you see him on the street, you won't forget him."

Andy moved the toothpick to the corner of his mouth. "Settin' up a bull ranch, is what I heard."

Charlie Dan said he had heard the same.

Finch came back into the conversation. "Is he a friend of O'Leary's?" he asked, in Henry's direction.

Henry had a flash memory of Windsor standing next to O'Leary in the saloon, and he remembered the strange laugh, but the impression had not yielded enough meaning to him, so he left it out of his answer. "As far as I know, he sold O'Leary a horse, and the horse went back to Windsor's, so he was returning it."

"Well," said Finch, "there's new people comin' into the country every day. What do you think of that, Fred?"

"I suppose it's all right."

Henry was not surprised to see Finch baiting the kid again. It was a familiar routine, the seasoned man of the world badgering the youngster. Sooner or later it always came around to women, and Finch now went on to do his part.

"You'd think they'd bring more women with 'em," he said. "What do you think of bein' out on the range for a month or two, Fred, and no women there?"

"I can get by."

Charlie Dan laughed. He had blond hair and a wavy blond mustache, and his mouth opened to a full, bright smile. "They'll keep you so busy you won't have time to think of girls."

Henry thought of Molly, her dark hair and dark eyes. He was pretty sure there was no way he'd be too busy to think about her, and he wasn't fond of not being able to ride in and see her for six weeks or more.

Andy shifted in his chair without saying anything. He took out the makings and rolled a cigarette. As he bent to his work, his pale bald head reminded Henry of a story.

Henry had never heard Andy tell the story, but the story was told about him and was supposed to be true.

A few years back, Andy had shown some interest in a young widow—a not very pretty widow, as the story went. She had a little baby, which Andy thought it was his duty to amuse. One day when he was dandling the baby on his lap, the baby knocked the hat off Andy's head. At the sight of the bald head, the baby started crying. Andy got the hat back on his head, and in a little while the baby was laughing again. After the episode with the widow, Andy did not seem to bother with women anymore, and woman talk around the bunkhouse went over him like water off a duck's back.

Henry moved his gaze from Andy to Finch. He wondered if Finch's pitter-patter about rustling and women was all for the kid's benefit or if some of it was double-barbed. Finch's poker face told him nothing.

Henry looked over at Fred. The kid had rolled up his right sleeve and now cocked his arm with the elbow up and the hand back by his ear. He moved his pipe to the left side of his mouth and put a nickel on his raised forearm. Then he gave his arm a jerk and snagged the nickel out of the air. He put two nickels on the forearm, hesitated, and took them off. He stood up, got the nickels into position again, and made a clean swipe of the two of them. After that he did three nickels, and then four. He did the trick with four nickels a couple of more times before he put the nickels away, sat down, and rolled his sleeve back down to cover his arm.

Henry wondered if Fred thought he was impressing the men or if it was his way of showing Finch that nothing he said bothered him. For Henry's own part, he thought the kid could use a kick in the seat of his pants, but he imagined something like that would happen before long anyway.

CHAPTER 7

HENRY SAT ON the sorrel and watched the herd below him. Jake had tried to kick him that morning as he reached under the horse's belly for the cinch, and he had picked up the offending hoof and had lifted it upward and outward for a long moment, putting pressure against the horse's hip to remind him how things were supposed to work. Now Jake stood like any other cow pony, still and relaxed with his head down.

From the high ground where he sat on the horse, Henry looked over the herd. It was the fifth day of roundup, and they had been making a good gather. Today he was taking his turn at day herding, a slow job but part of the work. The wagons and horse herd had already picked up and moved on toward the next camp, and in a little while, Henry and Charlie Dan would start to push the cattle in the same direction.

The sun had not risen very high but was already warming things up. Jake's reddish-brown neck glistened, and it was warm to the touch as Henry patted him. Jake would be glad to get on the move. Before long the flies would be out, and Jake was a good one at kicking and stamping, switching his tail, and throwing his head to keep off the flies.

Henry turned to his right and saw Cyrus Blaine riding his way from the general direction of where they had camped the night before. Cyrus kept a rifle in the bed wagon, and early that morning he had gone east with the gun. One of the Delmore riders had reported a coyote slinking after a late newborn calf, and the wild dogs had put up quite a yapping when the moon came up. Cyrus often took the trouble to go out after coyotes—and wolves too, on the rare occasions when they were reported. Henry had not heard any shots this morning, though, so he imagined Cyrus had not run into any luck.

As Cyrus rode up, Henry noticed the stock of the rifle sticking forward on the left side. It was a cumbersome thing on roundup, but the country was not very brushy, and as roundup boss, Cyrus could pick where he wanted to go.

As Cyrus reined up, he shook his head and smiled.

Henry put both his hands on the saddle horn. "No luck?"

"No yella dog." Cyrus took off his hat and dragged the cuff of his shirtsleeve across his forehead. He had short, light-colored hair that was going gray and thinning on top, so his pale scalp showed through for the moment he had his hat off. Then he put the hat back on—a dove-gray hat with a curled brim and a furrowed crown. Now he looked normal again, with the weathered hat matching the tan face, the gray eyes, and the crow's feet. "Gonna get hot," he said.

"Seems like it."

"Have you got any stragglers?" Cyrus looked across at the herd.

Henry shook his head. "They're all in pretty good shape so far."

Cyrus looked back at his rider. "Well, I'm gonna move on. Keep at it."

"You bet." Henry watched Cyrus ride away. Some bosses wouldn't have bothered to stop and say hello, but Cyrus usually did. Some men in his position forgot what it was like to work for wages, and some didn't. Cyrus was one who didn't. As a young man he had worked on the big railroad, the Union Pacific, and then he had gotten in on the early days of the cattle business in Wyoming. He rode and slept out with his men, and he always showed interest in whatever job he put them on. Some of the hands said he was that way because he had never gotten rich; others said he had never gotten rich because he was that way.

Henry sat for a while longer, and when he thought he'd like to move around, he spoke to Jake. The horse picked up its head, and Henry touched the spurs to him. Jake took out on a good walk, snorted a couple of times, and shook his head. Keeping to the higher ground, Henry rode around the herd to the other side, where Charlie Dan sat on a gray horse. He had his right leg hooked up over the saddle horn and his hat pushed back on his head, and he was chewing a stem of grass.

"Busy day," Henry said.

Charlie Dan nodded and yawned, then smoothed his mustache at the corners of his mouth.

"Maybe we can start to push 'em out when I get back to the other side."

"Might as well." Charlie Dan yawned again.

Henry laughed. "Did you go somewhere last night?" He and Charlie Dan had both ridden the night-herding shift from midnight till two.

"You know how it is. You ride hard for four days, and then you sit on your tail for a little while, and the body wants to go to sleep."

"Maybe you could get Fred to teach you a trick or two, maybe juggling, and you could practice that to help shorten the time and keep you awake."

Charlie Dan gave his full smile. "That kid's something, isn't he?"

"Hollis said he'd like to drag him behind the wagon for a day."

"Good way to stretch out a new rope."

They sat on their horses for a while longer, watching the herd; then Henry perked up his horse and pointed him back to where they had come from. A jackrabbit shot up out of the grass and gave Jake a scare for a second or two. Henry patted the horse on the neck and nudged him back on the job.

At camp that evening, another man joined the crew. He was Perry McCloud, a small-time rancher, who came to rep for his own brand. He brought a string of six good horses, including the one he rode. After dropping his bed and unsaddling his horse, he turned all six into the cavvy, or horse herd. Then he made his way to the chuck wagon.

McCloud was a tall, husky man with dark hair, dark brows, and a dark handlebar mustache. He wore a broad-brimmed black hat and a dark brown vest. Henry knew him from past roundups, knew that he lived alone and was known to be moody and not very talkative.

McCloud filled his plate and sat on the ground without saying much, just nodding or exchanging greetings as he had to. When he finished eating, he got up and carried his plate to the tailgate, where Fred was washing utensils. Then he came back to the same spot, sat down, and took out a pipe. Henry observed with satisfaction that it was a curved-stem pipe.

McCloud loaded the pipe and lit it, ground the match head under his boot heel, and looked at Henry. "I understand O'Leary is a friend of yours," he said.

Henry twisted his mouth. "Of sorts." He doubted that McCloud had been gossiping with Finch or that he would mention it if he had. Then, with what Henry hoped was a polite tone, he asked, "Any reason why you mention it?"

McCloud hooked his arms around his knees. "He gave you as a reference."

The sun was just setting, and most of the roundup crew was lounging around the fire. Henry had a sense of being in the public eye, and he imagined McCloud did too. So he waited for the other man to continue.

"He said he was going to a horse sale in Cheyenne, and

he talked me into letting him take a pair of horses." Mc-Cloud looked at the puncher on his left. "Good sleek horses, black geldings. Come out of their winter coat real nice. In good shape." He looked back at Henry. "I trained 'em as buggy horses, and they're gentle-broke for riding. I told him not to take less than two hundred dollars for the pair."

Henry raised his eyebrows and tipped his head to the side. "Well, that's between you and O'Leary."

"It is. But since he used your name, I thought I should tell you about it."

"I appreciate it."

For the next couple of days, Henry noticed that McCloud had little to say to him. McCloud was about forty, older than almost all the other riders, and he didn't talk much to anyone. Henry imagined he didn't like to deal with other people, since he lived alone and was not known for going to town very often. Now it seemed as if McCloud had second thoughts about letting O'Leary do the dealing for him and he was showing those thoughts by being sullen with Henry.

Since McCloud would probably be with the roundup for a week or even less, Henry figured he could take it in stride. He stayed out of the moody rancher's way, and he was glad to see McCloud pair up with Andy Galena. The riders usually rode out and came in in pairs, and even though McCloud seemed to be riding alone even then, he got along with Andy as well as he did with anyone else, except Cyrus Blaine. As a fellow rancher as well as roundup boss, Cyrus commanded McCloud's respect. And by splitting up Finch and Andy so that the latter could work with the dark lone wolf for the while that he would be in camp, Cyrus showed his understanding of men.

Although Henry didn't take McCloud's snubs personally, since the two of them really didn't know each other very well, he didn't like having been associated with

O'Leary in the way that McCloud had done it. If he was identified that way and then O'Leary went about his light-fingered business with other people's livestock, some of it could come back to roost with Henry.

After thinking it through several times, Henry decided to confer with Charlie Dan. He told the part about O'Leary's business proposition, but he left out what he had heard from O'Leary's wife. He wrapped up his account by saying, "So you can see why I don't like being made out to be one of his friends."

Charlie Dan widened his eyes. "That's for sure. He sounds like poison."

"Doesn't he, though?"

"And then this thing with McCloud's horses."

"I wish he hadn't used my name."

Charlie Dan shook his head. "Sounds to me like he's the kind of feller to stay away from."

"That's what I've decided, too."

On McCloud's second day with the roundup, the weather turned damp and drizzly. That made the ground slippery for horse and cattle work, so Cyrus called off any new work for the day. Hollis positioned the bed wagon and the chuck wagon end to end and about twelve feet apart. Then he brought out a large canvas fly and made a tent between the two wagons, where the punchers could dry out somewhat and keep from getting any wetter.

Most of the punchers had tepees, some round and some square, which stayed in the bed wagon most of the time. A few men had set theirs up before the ground got any wetter, while the rest preferred to wait and see if the bad weather cleared off. Over half the crew took cover under the large tent that Hollis had set up.

McCloud and Andy were on a four-hour shift holding the herd. Henry and Charlie Dan would be next, and they had their horses tied to the front left wheel of the chuck wagon. Henry could see them from where he sat. They were tied with hackamores, and each horse had a slicker draped over the saddle. The bridles were hung on the saddlehorns, under cover. If anything came up, at least two horses were at the ready.

Henry pulled the black thread through the eye of the needle and held the two strands against his right palm. It gave him a good feeling to look at the thread for a moment before he tied a knot in the end and went to work on a ripped shirt.

Charlie Dan was oiling his six-shooter, which he did not like to wear but which he took good care of. If he packed it at all, he had it in his saddlebag, and on roundup he left it in camp most of the time. It had gotten wet from the rain that had blown in through the end of the bed wagon, so he was tending to his equipment while he had the time.

A few other punchers were similarly engaged—two were mending clothes, one sharpening a knife, another oiling his gun after the example of Charlie Dan, and another wiping down a saddle. In the center of the tent, sitting on their bedrolls with a crate between them, sat three punchers playing dominoes. One was a rider from the Delmore, one was a 7–Bar cowpuncher, and one was Finch.

Smoke drifted in from the campfire, which Hollis kept going under another fly on the leeward side of the chuck wagon. The air under the tent had a full mixture of the smells of damp clothing, tobacco smoke, wood smoke, and gun oil. Only the three men playing dominoes did any talking.

"I hear McCloud has a brother who lives down south on Bear Creek," said the Delmore rider. "They say he's just like this one."

"Imagine that," said Finch, who liked table games and table talk.

The 7–Bar puncher, who was new to the country, said, "I thought Bear Creek was up north."

"There's more than one Bear Creek," said Finch as he laid down a tile. "There's as many creeks named Bear Creek in this country as there are ranchers named Wilson."

"Or wheat farmers named Johnson," added the Delmore hand.

"Them too," said Finch. "Swedes."

The Delmore rider laid down his piece. "Can you imagine them two together, the McClouds?"

"Yeah," said Finch. "I bet the jokes fly."

The weather cleared off that evening, and the next day was good for working. The boys finished the branding in late afternoon and put the herd on its evening ground. A couple of the younger punchers wanted to have some fun, so they suggested some steer wrestling. They said it was a good time to try it, because the ground was soft from the rain and nobody would get hurt.

By this time there were a few steers in the herd to choose from, so Henry and Charlie Dan roped out a two-year-old that had enough horns to grab onto. When they had the steer roped head and heels to a standstill, the puncher who wanted to try his stuff went to stand by the steer's head. Another man loosened Henry's rope from the horns while Charlie Dan shook his rope loose from the heels.

By now the contestant had his arms around the steer's head—right arm over the neck and hooking a horn, left arm cradling the steer's muzzle. Then the dance was on, with all the cowboys cheering as the man on the ground hopped and dug in his heels and finally flopped the steer over with its four feet in the air. The onlookers cheered and called for another as the steer got to its feet and sauntered away.

Henry and Charlie Dan roped out another steer like the first one, and the next puncher had his wrestling match. Then came a third steer, which ducked its head and left the cowboy sitting in the dirt. The fourth steer went belly-up like the first two, and then the punchers began calling for Fred.

The willowtail kid had shown some ability as a calf wrestler, one of two men who held down the front and rear ends of a calf while a third man did the branding, earmarking, and any other cuts that needed to be made. Some of the younger punchers had taken a liking to Fred, or at least liked to have fun with him. No doubt knowing he wanted to prove himself, they now called his name.

"He's too light in the ass to wrestle one of these," one of the boys said. "You wanna ride one, Fred?"

"I'll try it."

So Charlie Dan went into the herd and cut out a four-year-old that must have slipped through the net at shipping time the year before. He was a tall, rangy animal, not a true longhorn but a brindle fellow like many of them. He had horns about a foot long, so Henry swung a wide loop and caught him as he came out of the herd. Henry took his dallies and pulled the steer, bucking, until Charlie Dan caught the heels. Then they stretched the steer and put him on the ground.

Henry was on the blue roan, Dobber, and the two of them were turned around, facing the work. Fred had on a pair of spurs by now and was pulling a leather glove onto his left hand, while two other cowboys were pushing a length of rope under the front quarter of the steer. The animal lay wide-eyed and breathing hard through its nose, and its ribs heaved.

"Take two wraps," said one of the boys, a 7–Bar rider.

Finch came up as the kid settled down to straddle the steer. "Slide your left hand under the rope and take it in your fist," he said. "Then we'll snug 'er up."

The kid nodded and did as he was told.

Henry could see that the rope was a broken piece off the end of someone's lariat. It still had the loop, or hondo, which the boys positioned close to the top of the steer's shoulders. Then Finch ran the loose, tasseled end through the loop, pulled it snug, doubled the loose end, and made a slipknot.

"Hang on tight with your left hand," he said. "If this old boy doesn't throw you, and you want to get off, reach down with your right hand and grab this loose end, and pull it."

The kid nodded and pulled his hat down in front and back.

Finch and the other two cowboys backed away.

"Ready?" the 7–Bar rider called out as he leaned to loosen the rope around the horns.

"Yep."

"Turn 'er loose, then. Let 'er buck!"

The puncher flung the rope off the steer's horns, Charlie Dan eased up on the heels and shook loose, and the steer came up thrashing.

Hauling in his rope, Henry let Dobber back up and pull away. The steer bellowed and wheezed as it went into bucking, and the kid stayed on for the first two jumps. Then he went off the right side, with his left hand still hung up in the rope. His long, skinny arm was draped across the steer's shoulders, and his fluffy head jerked with every jump. His hat must have sailed off on the first bounce.

It looked as if the kid either couldn't or didn't remember to reach across for the loose end of the slipknot. The steer was turning into him now, trying to hook the foreign thing with a horn and get it off him. Fred was still hung up, flopping up and down like a foot rug someone was shaking at the back door.

Not five seconds had gone by, and Henry had his rope gathered up. He shook out a new loop, spurred Dobber in, and slapped the rope around the steer's nose and left horn. That was probably the best he was going to do.

Meanwhile, Charlie Dan had pulled in his own rope and was getting set to try to catch the heels again. Henry saw the loop go down out of sight, and then he saw Charlie Dan give a pull and the slack of the rope coming back at him. He had missed. Now he was quick-gathering for a second try.

The steer had its head twisted against Henry's rope, and it was pulling back and still thrashing. Henry knew he didn't have a good catch, but he hoped it would hold.

Then McCloud appeared at the steer's left side, the tall rancher quick and dark, moving with the steer. Henry saw the quick flash of a blade, which would be McCloud's sharp marking knife. Both new ends of the rope popped away from the steer's hunched shoulder, and the gloved hand went up and then out of view.

Henry pulled the steer away, shook the loop until it came off, and then with the help of Charlie Dan he hazed the steer back to the herd. Neither of them said a word, just raised their eyebrows as they straightened out the coils and tied down their ropes.

When they got back to what had been the rodeo ground, Fred was on his feet. He was holding his left arm, with the leather glove palm up, close to his body, while his right hand hung at his side holding his hat. His face showed pain.

"Did he hook you?" Henry asked.

"No, but he jerked the hell out of me."

Serves you right, Henry thought, but he said nothing. He looked around for McCloud and saw the tall, dark form riding back to the chuck wagon.

"I bet he's mad," said Charlie Dan.

The kid looked around as he put his hat on his head. "Called me a damn fool." Then he gave a pained smile. "He's probably right."

CHAPTER 8

CYRUS BLAINE HAD stayed at the chuck wagon with Hollis while the boys had their fun. When Charlie Dan and Henry came to camp he asked no questions, and Henry imagined that a few words from McCloud had told him as much as he wanted to know.

Fred turned out to be not very badly damaged, but he did show some bruises on his lower legs where the steer had managed to kick him in between flops. Henry thought that the worst outcome of the incident was Fred's attitude. The kid apparently now felt he had proven himself to some degree, for the Delmore puncher who had lent him the spurs let him keep them. "For being a good sport," he said. Henry wished the other lads wouldn't humor Fred that way—or if they did, he wished they would have to live with him afterward.

To his credit, Fred did not wear the spurs when he washed dishes and gathered wood. However, a couple of days after the steer riding, he asked Cyrus Blaine when he was going to get to ride.

Cyrus's answer, in front of Henry and a few others, was simple and polite. "When I think you're ready."

On the day after that, the crew was gathered at the chuck wagon for the midday meal when Henry saw a rider coming from the southeast. It was not unusual to see another rider, as visitors frequently came and went. To see someone arriving at mealtime was quite normal, for the code of the cow country was open and hospitable.

Henry did not pay close attention until the rider had come within a couple of hundred yards, at which distance he could then see that the rider was Van O'Leary. He was riding the bay horse, which meant he had been home at least long enough to change horses. Henry made quick work of the rest of his plate of food, put his plate and silverware in the wreck pan, and walked to the edge of camp. A few of the other punchers were paying attention now, and Henry could feel a knot in his stomach.

About fifty yards out from the camp, the bay horse began to pitch, as if it was determined one more time to get the burden off its back. Then the horse settled down, and Henry could see that O'Leary was sawing on the reins. The horse came on a little farther and began to throw its head and shake its bridle. Henry watched as O'Leary jerked on the reins to make the horse stop and back up. The horse began to sidestep and wave its head, and then Henry saw something he did not like.

O'Leary had untied his rope from the saddle, and with the knotted loose end he began to beat the horse on the top of the head, between the ears. The horse lifted its head and opened its mouth, and O'Leary rapped it a few more times as he jerked on the reins. Finally the horse settled down again, and the rider rapped it again, apparently just for good measure. Then he rode the horse into camp, dismounted, and tied the reins to the right rear wheel of the bed wagon. He gave no indication that the little exhibition had taken place, but came strolling up to Henry with his usual jaunty demeanor.

"I see you made it back," Henry said.

"Safe and sound. I was passin' by, so I thought I'd drop in and say hello."

"You'd better take on some grub. You don't want to hurt the cook's feelings."

O'Leary smiled and his head swayed. "I'm glad you reminded me."

Henry felt uneasy at being seen with O'Leary, but since he felt responsible for the man's presence in camp, he said, "I'll have a cup of coffee and keep you company."

"Sounds fine."

As O'Leary turned toward the chuck wagon, Henry asked, "Wife all right?"

"Just fine, thanks. And thanks for the lookout."

"I really didn't do anything."

"Well, thanks all the same."

"Any time."

All of a sudden O'Leary stopped, and Henry saw why. McCloud had just left his horse with the day wrangler and was walking to the wagon. O'Leary seemed to hesitate; then he continued toward the grub.

McCloud walked right past them and without looking, said, by way of greeting, "O'Leary."

"Howdy."

O'Leary got a plate of grub and sat on the ground, and Henry poured himself a cup of coffee and sat nearby. He had lost track of McCloud for a moment, until the tall man appeared at the chuck wagon and began to serve himself a plate of beans and beefsteak. McCloud sat on the ground about five yards from O'Leary and at a right angle from him.

Henry could feel the attention of the other cowhands. McCloud ate in silence for a few minutes and then spoke without looking directly at O'Leary. "Looks like you're back from your business trip."

"That I am. As they say in the Bible, I am back resting under my own vine and my own fig tree."

McCloud looked at him and then looked back at his plate. "And how did it go?"

"About the way things can."

"Does that mean good or bad?"

"Not as good as either of us might have hoped."

"What does that mean in black and white?"

O'Leary looked at McCloud without a trace of nervousness and said, "I got a hundred for the two of them."

"You mean a hundred each."

"No, I mean a hundred altogether."

McCloud set down his plate. It looked as if he was going to get up, but instead he turned and supported himself with his right hand on the ground. "I told you not to take any less than a hundred each. That's the least they were worth. You should have been able to get that anywhere."

O'Leary mopped at his plate with a biscuit. "You told me to get the best price I could, and I did."

McCloud took his knife, which he had been using to cut beefsteak, from his plate and wiped it on the cuff of his trousers. He folded it, leaned back, put it in his pocket, and leaned again on his right hand. "I can't believe you only got a hundred dollars."

Henry marveled at O'Leary's brashness as he said, "Are you saying you don't believe me?"

That was the ultimate taunt: Call me a liar, and then be prepared to back it up with proof or force.

Henry had no doubt that McCloud could back it up with his fists or any weapon, but the rancher paused. "Not necessarily," he said, "because you just might be that stupid."

O'Leary remained unruffled. "If I used any poor judgment, it must have been when I offered to help you out to begin with."

McCloud looked at him and said nothing, but Henry could see the hatred building in his face.

O'Leary set down his plate and licked his fingers. "It's done," he said, "and there's no undoin' it. And you will get your money."

"Oh, I will? When?"

"I don't have it on me."

"Why don't you run home to your fig tree and get it? You could be back by nightfall."

"I don't have it. That trip cost me money, and most of that hundred got eat up in expenses."

McCloud was leaning toward O'Leary by now, and he was nearly shouting. "You don't have it? You sold my two horses, which are better than anything you'll ever own, and you don't even have the money!"

O'Leary gave him a cold stare. "I told you, I'll *pay* you. It's not as if I was trying to beat you out of it."

McCloud got up, picking up his plate as he did, and walked over to stand in front of O'Leary. "I could kick your face in."

"It won't get you your money any sooner."

McCloud turned and walked away. He handed his plate to Fred without stopping and went back to the horse herd.

O'Leary looked at Henry and said, "I can't help it. I'm in a pinch worse than he is, and I'll get the money to him as soon as I can."

Henry wanted to say that he thought O'Leary had a poor way of doing business, but he thought better of it and said, "It's between you two."

The other cowhands, who had been more or less frozen in place by the altercation between the two men, were now rising from the ground and filing away. Henry shook the grounds out of his tin cup and said, "I should be gettin' back to work, too."

O'Leary smiled. "Don't let me keep you. I think I'd like to bum a second plate of grub, but I can do that on my own."

A little later on, after Henry and Charlie Dan had saddled up and were riding away from camp, Henry said, "Could you believe that?"

Charlie Dan gave him a wide-eyed look and shook his head. "Reminds me of the sayin' about the fella that lies so bad, he has to have his wife call the dog."

Henry felt a little stab at the mention of the wife, but he knew there was nothing in it. He said, "For a while there I thought McCloud was going to do more than he did."

"So did I."

*   *   *

O'Leary was long gone when the men rode back in at the end of the day, and McCloud seemed to have cooled down. He sat around the fire with the rest of the crew, and although he didn't say anything, he smoked his pipe and listened as the talk went around.

Jimmy, the Delmore puncher who had been playing dominoes a few days earlier, said he had come up with a song. He looked at Finch and said, "After our little joke the other day, I've had this song runnin' through my head. I even sang it to the cows."

Finch straightened out his vest and said, "Well, let's hear it."

Jimmy looked around. Several of the other hands chimed in, telling him to do his song. He stood up by the campfire, a handsome young cowpuncher in his mid-twenties, with sandy brown hair, blue eyes, and a clear, smiling face. He set his hat back on his head and hooked his thumbs in his vest pockets.

"We don't have any music," he said. "But we're used to that. Here it goes. I call it 'Song of the Flaxen-Haired Maiden.' " Then, in a steady voice, he sang the song:

> A flaxen-haired maiden from Sweden
> Stepped down from the train in Cheyenne.
> She said, "I'm a wheat farmer's sweetheart.
> I've come here to marry my man.
>
> "I love him though I've never met him,
> His photograph I've never seen—
> But here I am now in this city,
> To be his sweet bride at sixteen.
>
> "He's written me long, lovely letters
> About the big farm he has here—
> One hundred and twenty-five acres,
> And six months' vacation each year.
>
> "He tells me I'll find it delightful
> Where winters are generally warm—

So please, if you can, won't you tell me
The way to the Johnson farm?"

A round of applause, with laughter, followed Jimmy's delivery.

"You made that up yourself?" asked a 7–Bar rider.

"I couldn't help it," said Jimmy, laughing. "It kept runnin' through my head till I had it pieced together."

"I like the part about the six-month vacation," said Charlie Dan. "What he didn't tell her was that out here, it's six months of flies and six months of winter."

"She'll get an education pretty fast, once she meets him," said Finch.

All the cowboys laughed, and Henry saw that even McCloud had half a smile on his face.

The next day's work called for another circle ride, or wide sweep of the country to gather cattle. Henry had thoughts of making a circle horse out of Jake, but today's would be a big circle ride that would call for all the riders except the day herders. For such a hard ride, Henry picked a solid black horse out of his string. It was a dependable, short-coupled mount with good wind, and he hadn't ridden it for a few days. As he brushed the horse and saddled it, he thought of McCloud's two black horses and how infuriating it must be for McCloud to feel swindled by someone as cheeky as O'Leary. Any man appreciated a good horse, and to lose two of them—Henry didn't blame McCloud for being angry.

His thoughts went again to O'Leary, and he wondered why the man took the bother to ride all the way out to the cow camp. He imagined it was probably just to test the water—to see what sort of reaction he might get out of Henry. It was a good bet he didn't expect to see McCloud, and he almost did get his face kicked in. He should count himself lucky.

Henry turned the idea over again. There was also the

possibility that O'Leary was using the visit as an excuse to look over the country and have a look at the calf crop. Henry laughed to himself. That—and eat a bellyful of someone else's beef.

As Henry went to put the bridle on the horse, he brushed his hand across its nose and felt the stubs of cactus spines. He could not see the needles very well in the dim morning light, so he slipped the halter back on the horse, looped the bridle on the saddle horn, and led the horse to the chuck wagon. There he tied it to a wheel, and by the light of Hollis's lantern that hung from a pole on the wagon, he pulled the spines from the black horse's nose. Then he put on the bridle, tightened the cinch, checked to see that his slicker was tied down, and swung up into the saddle. He touched the rope at his right knee, adjusted his reins, and rode back into the gray light and cool smell of the morning.

As usual, the riders went out in pairs, heading in the direction Cyrus told them. Cyrus had been with the herd during O'Leary's visit the day before, and there was no telling whether any word of the incident had come his way. Generally the men did not tell tales on one another to the big boss, especially if it was a personal bicker. Henry knew there were stool pigeons on some ranches, but Cyrus had never encouraged favor seeking on the Box Elder, so unless an incident concerned Cyrus or the ranch, the men did not go out of their way to report it. In spite of the discretion, though, Cyrus had a good sense of where there was compatibility or animosity. As Henry had heard him say, he "drank the same coffee and soaked up the same woodsmoke." Henry was not surprised, then, when Cyrus sent him and Charlie Dan to the opposite end of the drive from McCloud and Andy.

After he had ridden to the far point and split up from Charlie Dan, Henry thought again of O'Leary. Henry wondered if the red-haired man carried a running iron beneath his saddle skirt. On those ranches where the company was king and no hired man could own his own stock, some men had the attitude that they had to look out for themselves. They might try to get set up on their own, or go silently with a partner who didn't ride for a brand, or shuffle a few head to a free operator like O'Leary. Those were the men who were on the lookout for a draw or hidey-hole where they could hog-tie a calf, build a quick little sagebrush fire, and burn some hair. Such men would carry a running iron. Henry doubted that any of the Box Elder hands would be up to that game. For his own part, he was content to draw summer wages and feel he had nothing to hide. It was a good feeling to be free under the open sky and not have to look over his shoulder.

Then he thought about Molly. Whether she turned out to be the one for him or not, the woman who joined her life with his deserved a free life, too. She shouldn't have to live a life of worry. He imagined that a woman like Dora felt anxious every time she saw the approach of the distant dark form of a horse and rider.

That evening, at the end of the long day's gather, Henry found the camp where Hollis had said it would be. As Henry turned the black horse over to Al, the wrangler, he was met with a quiet voice.

"There's goin' to be hell to pay, I bet," Al said.

"What for?"

"That kid Fred got into the herd today and put a hacka-more on McCloud's roan and tried to ride it."

Henry flinched and then shook his head. No one rode a horse out of another man's string without his say-so, not a company horse and especially not a man's own horse. "Did he know whose it was?"

"I don't think so. I think he tried that one because it was the only one he could catch. It bucked him off right away, anyway."

"Does McCloud know?"

"He hasn't come in yet, but I think Hollis is gonna tell him."

Henry gave a low whistle. "There *will* be hell to pay."

Charlie Dan and Henry were seated on the ground a few yards from the fire when McCloud came to the wagon. Henry saw Hollis take McCloud away from the tailgate, where Fred was grinding coffee. When they came back, McCloud stood off from the wagon, at the edge of the light cast by the lantern and fire, and called out loud.

"Boy, come here."

Fred turned around and quit grinding.

"You. Fred. Get over here."

Fred walked over and faced him. Henry thought the kid should look more worried.

"I understand you tried to ride a horse of mine today."

Fred grinned. "Not for long."

McCloud's right hand came around, broad and open, and caught the side of Fred's face. Then the left hand came around and slapped him again. The kid's hat flew away as he staggered backward. McCloud stepped forward and slapped him again with the right, and Fred hit the ground. As he got up on all fours, McCloud leaned over him and smacked him three more times, all of them loud whacks with the open hand—right, left, right—until the kid rolled over on his stomach and covered the sides of his face with his arms.

McCloud stood still. "Maybe that'll teach you not to touch another man's horse."

Cyrus appeared at the edge of the light. "McCloud's right, sonny. Look up at me."

The kid did as he was told.

"There was a time, and there still is in some places, when you could get shot for that kind of stunt. Now I'm goin' to ask you to roll your blankets and get gone. I'll get Al to take you into town, and he can be back in time for his shift in the morning. I'll tell him to saddle the horses, and while you're gettin' your things together, I'll draw up your pay." Cyrus turned to McCloud. "You know, Perry, you didn't have to go that far."

McCloud nodded and walked away. After Fred had picked himself up and taken his hat with him, McCloud came back into the light and served himself a plate of grub.

Henry figured Cyrus had done well. He was getting the troublemaker out of camp, and he was letting Al lose a night's sleep. Al may or may not have had anything to do with Fred's transgression, but it had happened when he was in charge of the horse herd. Henry thought, *If you hadn't been with the crows, you wouldn't have been shot at.*

When the hoofbeats of the two horses had faded and the two young men were safely gone and out of hearing, Hollis stood by the fire with a cup of coffee. Cyrus had gone to his tent, and the atmosphere was relaxed. After a moment or two of silence, Hollis said, "There's only so much you should have to put up with from a damn kid."

Henry looked at Finch, who was trimming his fingernails and not looking up from beneath the heavy eyebrows. Then he looked at Charlie Dan, who turned down the corners of his mouth and nodded.

Hollis spoke again. "That kid sniveled to Cyrus and cadged a job to begin with. But you can't blame Cyrus. He was trying to give the kid a break. But I'm damn sure glad to be done with him."

In a little while, Henry and Charlie Dan got up. They had first relief, the night-herding shift from ten till midnight, so they dropped their tin cups in the pan and left the camp.

At the edge of the horse herd, Charlie Dan spoke in a low voice. "I think Cyrus was right. McCloud didn't have to go that far."

"Meanin' he should have just slapped the kid once or twice."

Charlie Dan laughed.

Henry said, "That just goes to show you. A week ago, I would have picked Finch to do that little piece of work."

"You might have missed your bet by only a day. I think McCloud was plannin' to leave after tomorrow anyway."

That night, as Henry rode the edges of the bed ground, he looked up at the stars and thought it wouldn't be all that bad a night to ride to town. He didn't usually think about town when he was out and away from it, but the thought of the two young men riding across the country under the stars reminded him that there was a town. It was just Willow Creek, but in a house in that town, under these same stars, a pretty girl with dark hair was probably just going to sleep.

CHAPTER 9

HENRY SAT IN the shade of the sorrel horse, Jake. The herd spread out below him for a half mile in the rolling grass country. The animals were grazing, but from this distance the scene looked motionless. The sun overhead had not seemed to move in the last hour, and the land stretched away forever in all directions. Although there was almost always some breeze or stronger wind in this part of Wyoming, the afternoon was almost breathless.

Time seemed to stand still, with one day a replica of the day before, but there were signs of the summer marching on. The flies were getting worse, especially when the outfit camped near water, which it almost always did. The prickly pear cactus had bloomed for its season, and now the yellow silk flowers had wilted and passed away. Henry knew that on one of those days now gone, the wild roses at his cabin had finished blooming for the season. The days now became a little shorter, barely noticeable, but the longest day of the year had come and gone, and the sun was moving back south.

The roundup crew was at its farthest point north and west, and tomorrow would be the last day. They would brand the last bunch, turn out the animals that would continue to graze here, and drive back the animals they were herding—cattle that the crew was holding for other ranches and cattle that the three roundup outfits wanted closer to their home ranches.

It had been a good season so far. After Fred and McCloud were gone, the roundup stayed hectic as always but was not burdened by personal trouble. Other reps came and went, and the roundup went on smoothly. It called for long days and hard work without a day off, but when a man followed the wagon, life had a reason and an order to it, a sense of achievement and destination.

Not everything was perfect, though. Henry had not been able to make a good circle horse out of Jake, so he had used the sorrel for day herding and short jobs. As in the past couple of years, Dobber was the best calf-roping horse in Henry's string, but he knew that Dobber was over twelve years old, and ranch horses in this country did not last as long as a stabled horse in town did. The blue roan still had the pep and the quickness, but his back was beginning to sway, and Henry knew that the horse would not last forever.

Henry was aware the same could be said about himself. Here at midsummer the season seemed endless, as if long days would follow one another without change. But he knew that every day finished was a day gone, and the season would end, too. That long-gone, long-haired kid named Fred had been in square underwear when Henry bought his first saddle, and half the cattle on the ranch had been born since Henry came to Wyoming. With a little luck he would outlive old Jake here, and Dobber, and his own good horse, Beau. How and when he himself would go to "the last roundup"—or "beyond the sunset," as some of the boys said—he did not know, but he knew it would happen at some point. It might come when a good fast horse, like the black horse he had named Rocket, put his foot in a badger hole. Or it could come when he was an old man with toothless gums and sunken cheeks, mumbling about the days when a man rode for his pay.

There was no sense worrying about it; he had made his mind up about that. But it helped to remember once in a while that a fellow didn't know how much of life was left, on the basis of how much he had lived already. He just hoped there was a fair amount of green pasture ahead.

He smiled. In a few days they would be back under the roof of the Box Elder bunkhouse, with a few free days ahead of them. He knew he would spend some of that time checking on his place at Ruby Canyon, and some of it checking on Molly.

Back at the Box Elder headquarters, the three outfits made ready to split the cattle herd and the horse herd. The Delmore riders would go back to their ranch, and the 7–Bar riders would go back to theirs. All the cowhands were parting on friendly terms and with the expectation of getting together for fall roundup in a couple of months.

Before the outfits split up, however, they made a last camp at the Box Elder. With all the cattle and horses put away in a pasture for the evening, the men had no night-herding duties, so they enjoyed a relaxed atmosphere. Another rider from the Delmore had come to help drive back the cattle and horses, and two men who were surveying for the state also shared the camp for the night. Hollis fed them all, and well. Now that he was back at his own cook house, he put out potatoes and onions as well as fried beefsteak, gravy, and biscuits. To top it off, and to send everyone away with a good impression of the Box Elder fare, he turned out six pies from his store of dried apples.

During this festivity, Henry and Andy kept busy shuffling food and dishes back and forth. Charlie Dan was laid up with a toothache, and Hollis provided him with a sedative that in other instances went by the name of snake-bite medicine. Finch, who was nominally in charge of the corrals and pastures for the time, lounged in the camp and gossiped. When the other two outfits had pulled out, then, he had a good supply of what could loosely be called information. Until the other Box Elder hands made it to town and got to hear it for themselves, it qualified as news.

When the last of the outsiders were gone and the stock had been tended to, the Box Elder hands lounged in the bunkhouse with the door open. Charlie Dan was still laid up, so Andy smoked by himself at the doorway as Finch began to parcel out the news.

"Well," he said, looking at Henry from where he lay sprawled out on his bunk, "it seems like your sorrel-headed friend has gone to work for Windsor."

"Is that right." Henry made it a statement as much as a question, hoping not to encourage any talk that would associate him with either O'Leary or Windsor.

"That's what I heard."

"Uh-huh."

Andy licked his upper lip and made a dry spit. "Isn't Windsor the one who's supposed to be starting a bull ranch?"

Finch spoke again. "Yes, sir. Except I haven't heard about him getting any bulls. Have you, Henry?"

"I really don't know anything about him."

"But you've met him. That's more than the rest of us have done."

"Yes, I've met him, but I didn't ask him about his business."

"Business is what it is."

"Is that right."

Finch put his hands together in back of his head and crossed his boots. "What I heard."

Andy made a half-smile as he took the wet cigarette from his mouth. "Well, let's have it."

Finch's eyes darted from Andy to Henry as he began. "Well, I got this from the Delmore rider first. You know, this fella Windsor likes to make a show around town, buyin' this thing and that, and always payin' with twenty-dollar gold pieces."

"I've heard that," said Andy.

"Thing is, he doesn't buy anything big. Talks about what he's gonna buy, but really doesn't spend all that much money." Finch gave one of his smug smiles and went on.

"Well, it seems that every so often he takes the stage down to Cheyenne, and takes all his change with him, and converts it into a new supply of twenty-dollar gold pieces."

Andy spit out a fleck of tobacco. "I'll be damned."

"The Delmore rider said a couple different people from town have seen him down there in Cheyenne and picked up on it. The two surveyors said they had heard it, too, that there was some showboat from up this way that went down there to trade in his small change."

"Makes you wonder," said Andy.

"Sure does." Finch smiled at Henry. "Makes you wonder if O'Leary'll get paid."

Henry licked his lips. "It's his problem if he doesn't."

Finch's eyes sparkled. "Or McCloud's."

Henry washed clothes that afternoon and got ready to take a few days on his own. Then the next morning he saddled Beau and rode cross-country to his homestead. When he got there, everything looked the same as when he had left it, except that the wild roses were well out of bloom and now had hard little dark orange globes. He remembered seeing a few of the fruitlike pieces floating in the horse trough the year before—dropped by magpies, which were handy at carrying dead freight. Looking around, he saw the corral, woodpile, and firepit all the same.

Inside the dugout, which was dry and cool and dusty, he saw no evidence of anybody having made use of the place. Dust had sifted from the roof onto the coffee, flour, rice, and other items he had left on the hanging shelf, and a couple of dead moths lay in the dust. He ducked under the bag of clothing and came to the hanging bundle of burlap. Wiggling his hand into the end, he satisfied himself that the rifle was still there. He gave the cabin another look around and, seeing nothing to raise his interest, walked back out into the daylight and closed the door.

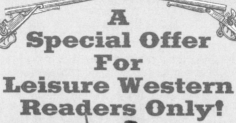

GET YOUR 4 FREE* BOOKS NOW— A VALUE OF BETWEEN $17 AND $20

Mail the Free* Books Certificate Today!

FREE* BOOKS CERTIFICATE!

YES! I want to subscribe to the Leisure Western Book Club. Please send me my 4 FREE* BOOKS. Then, each month, I'll receive the four newest Leisure Western Selections to preview for 10 days. If I decide to keep them, I will pay the Special Member's Only discounted price of just $3.36 each, a total of $13.44 ($16.35 in Canada). This saves me between $3 and $6 off the bookstore price. There are no shipping, handling or other charges.* There is no minimum number of books I must buy and I may cancel the program at any time. In any case, the 4 FREE* BOOKS are mine to keep—at a value of between $17 and $20!

*In Canada, add $7.50 US shipping and handling per order for first shipment. For all subsequent shipments to Canada the cost of membership in the Book Club is $16.35 US plus $7.50 US shipping and handling per order. All payments must be made in US dollars.

Name _____

Address _____

City_____ State_____

Zip_____ Telephone_____

Signature_____

Biggest Savings Offer!

For those of you who would like to pay us in advance by check or credit card—we've got an even bigger savings in mind. Interested? Check here. ☐

If under 18, parent or guardian must sign. Terms, prices and conditions subject to change. Subscription subject to acceptance. Leisure Books reserves the right to reject any order or cancel any subscription.

Tear here and mail your FREE* book card today!

Get Four Books Totally
F R E E* –
A Value of between
$16 and $20

Tear here and mail your FREE* book card today!

PLEASE RUSH
MY FOUR FREE*
BOOKS TO ME
RIGHT AWAY!

LeisureWestern Book Club
P.O. Box 6613
Edison, NJ 08818-6613

With nothing to keep him for the moment, he could go into Willow Creek.

The midday sun was pouring down its warmth as Beau brought them to the edge of town. As they passed the house where Henry had seen the clump of blue flax blooming in the spring, he saw that those flowers, too, had run their season. Now the long slender stalks were drooping with the weight of tan beads the size of the smallest peas. That was good, he thought, for each little ball would have dark seeds for future seasons.

The town had some activity on the main street, as evidenced by the number of wagons with horses standing in harness, as well as by the saddle horses standing at the hitch racks and swishing flies. Other outfits would be coming off roundup by now, also, so people would be driving in from the ranches to buy supplies. And, of course, the scrubbed and suntanned riders like himself would have come to buy new bandanas and hear the tinkle of music and gentle laughter.

When he entered the mercantile, he saw that Molly was busy with two ranch women, who had a heap of items on the counter. He caught her glance and then went back outside to sit on the bench. As he sat gazing, he saw a wagon being pulled by four mules. He did not recognize the driver, and the load was covered by a heavy canvas tarpaulin. Henry imagined it was a load of supplies on the way to a work camp, and he remembered Finch saying that a crew of ditch graders had come to the area.

After a little while, the bell on the door sounded and the two women walked out with their bundles. When they had moved down the sidewalk a few steps, Henry got up and went inside.

Molly looked at him and smiled, but he wished he could have seen more sparkle in that first moment. "Hello, Henry," she said.

He put as much cheer as he could into his voice. "Hello, Molly."

"Can I help you with something today? It looks as if you're back from roundup."

"I sure am."

"Everything went well?"

"Well enough. We finished out fine."

"That's good." She paused, and Henry did not sense the playfulness he remembered from the earlier visits. She took a small breath and asked, "And is there something I can help you find?"

"Well—um, no, not really. I just dropped in to say hello."

"That was thoughtful of you." She smiled, but it looked as if some uneasiness lay behind the smile.

"It's been a while," he said.

"Yes, it has."

"So I just thought I would stop in."

"I'm glad you did."

For a moment, it seemed as if there were a pane of glass between them. He noticed she was wearing a lavender dress, one solid color as before, but instead of feeling that the person in the dress had a life or spirit that touched with his, he felt she was a being apart—something he couldn't touch.

"Well," he said, "I should probably move along. I don't want to keep you." He hesitated, shifting his left foot as if to turn.

She looked away and then back at him. "I don't mean to make you feel that way."

Now their eyes met. He wanted to ask if she had a caller, but he couldn't think of a way to phrase the question and not feel stupid, so he asked, "Is there something wrong?"

"I don't know," she answered.

Words came to him. "What is it?"

Her eyes were glossy. "It's not something I should be

talking about here." She moved her head in the direction of the back of the store.

"Do you think we could meet a little later on?"

She arched her eyebrows. "At six?"

That seemed like forever, but he said, "Sure. That would be fine."

"You know where I'm staying, don't you?"

He nodded, picturing the house.

"I'm sure it would be all right if we sat on the front porch," she said.

He saw the porch in his mind. It faced north. There would be some shade. "That sounds good. I can see you then."

Her right hand went up and brushed loose hair from her cheekbone. Then she put her hands together at her waist. "At six, then, or a little after?"

"I'll look forward to it."

The first half hour went all right, as Henry sat for a haircut. Then for the next five and a half hours he fidgeted. He took Beau for a drink, tied him back up, and a little while later moved him to a spot where a taller false front cast the first of the afternoon shade. In the cafe next to the hotel he ate a bowl of stew and drank two cups of coffee. After that he went out and walked, then returned to the hotel lobby and glanced through an Omaha newspaper. He even wrote a short letter to his mother and father in Kansas and walked to the post office to send it. Finally the clock in the hotel lobby read a quarter to six, so he went out and untied Beau. He didn't want to cross paths with Molly when she got off work because he wanted to see her at the appointed time and place, so he took a ride out beyond the edge of town. On his way back, he meandered up and down a few streets that ran north and south, until he looked down the proper cross street and saw Molly sitting on the porch.

As he tied his horse and walked up to the porch, he felt restraint in the atmosphere again. Molly greeted him sitting down, and their hands touched for an instant. Henry took off his hat and kept it in his hand as he sat in the armless chair near her.

In the course of the afternoon he had thought of a thousand things to say. Now in the warm shade of the porch, he heard himself say, "I have the feeling that something has happened."

She looked at her hands and then at him, her face wincing. "I met someone. Someone I don't care for a great deal."

"Uh-huh."

"He says he knows you." She paused. "He says you know his wife."

He envisioned a flash of sorrel hair and a laughing face. "Van O'Leary."

"Yes."

"Well, I hope you don't think he's a great friend of mine."

She was looking at her lap again. "Not from the things he said."

Henry felt his heartbeat quicken. "What did he have to say?"

"Well, he talks quite a bit, as you probably know. But there's one thing he said, more than once, that was not kind."

"I suppose I'd better hear it."

"He said . . . that you didn't have any respect for marriage."

A jolt went through him. "He what? He said that!" He recalled the picture of the yellow-haired saloon girl, plus the shadowy image of the woman in Kentucky. "As if he should talk!" Henry raised his hat and lowered it, then looked at Molly. "Was he referring to my visiting his wife while he was gone, just before I left for the ranch?"

Her face was clear now, and she nodded.

"Well, he *asked* me to go check on her. I didn't want to, but I did. And then she asked me to come back." Molly's face seemed to fall, so he said quickly, "I didn't even go inside the house. I was careful about that. All I did was talk—or mainly listen."

Molly nodded.

Henry took a breath. "And I'll tell you—well, I can't tell you in detail what she said—but I'll tell you this. If there's someone who hasn't got any respect for marriage, it's him."

"Oh, I could see that."

Henry's brow furrowed. "Oh?"

"He asked me if I'd like to meet him somewhere."

Henry felt his free hand clench. "Whoa!" he said. "What a hypocrite!"

"That's what it seemed like to me."

"But you thought there might be something to the other part?"

"I didn't know."

"What a mangy little vermin!" His thought went inward for a second, and then his eyes met hers again. "Did you think that maybe he was playing up to you as a sort of turn-about?"

"I think he tried to make it seem that way."

"Do you mind if I ask what you thought about it? I mean, what did you really think?"

Her hands moved in her lap but did not go anywhere. "To tell you the truth, I didn't know what to think. I thought there was something wrong with his story, but I didn't know what, and I wondered why you might have been friends with him in the first place."

"I'll tell you, he's no friend of mine."

"I wouldn't think so, after this."

They talked for a little while longer, until Molly went in for supper. Henry unhitched Beau and decided to walk, leading the horse. He needed time to think. He knew he was going to look for O'Leary, but in the meanwhile he wanted to think about how he stood with Molly.

Even in the latter part of their conversation, he hadn't seen the sparkle from before. Still, he thought, she hadn't closed the curtain on him, and she could have. That was a good sign. She was willing to talk to him and face him with what she had heard. She had also been willing to be seen with him on the front porch—and given the looseness of O'Leary's tongue and the quickness of gossip in a small town, that in itself was an expression of confidence.

Although he had resolved himself earlier to avoid both of the O'Learys if possible, Henry now found himself inquiring in the Gold Eagle. There he learned that O'Leary had been in the habit of coming to town two or three nights a week. He hadn't made an appearance in the Gold Eagle since Saturday, and this being a Wednesday, there was a good chance that he might darken the door.

Henry moved his horse down the street and went into the cafe for a bit of supper. Still on edge, but more out of anger than nervousness now, he killed time until the sun went down. Then he left the cafe. As he walked back down the board sidewalk, he spotted the bay horse in front of the Gold Eagle. He felt his stomach tighten, and with each hand he rubbed his thumb against his fingers.

O'Leary was seated at the bar in about the same place where Henry had found him the first time. He had a bottle of whiskey in front of him. Henry stopped at the end of the bar and called for a glass of beer, which he preferred anyway. Then he moved down the bar and stood next to O'Leary.

Each man had a hand on his drink, and neither made a motion toward shaking hands.

"Hello, Henry."

"Hello, Van. Been a while."

O'Leary turned and smiled. "It has."

"I heard you went to work for Windsor."

O'Leary tipped his head as if looking up at the elk antlers, then puffed his cheeks and spit into the cuspidor. As he turned back to face Henry, he swayed his head and smiled. "Gotta keep the wolf from the door."

"Uh-huh."

O'Leary looked around the saloon. "There's a little boom in business right now."

"Some."

O'Leary looked back at his drink. "Did you just get in?"

"Earlier in the day." Henry took a drink of beer. It was cold and tasted good, but he felt like flinging it in O'Leary's face. It galled him to see the man acting as if all was normal. He set down his beer and said, "I got to do a little visiting."

O'Leary held his tongue between his lips and then opened his mouth. "In town here?"

"Yes. With that girl you saw me talking to a while back."

O'Leary held his head up slightly and looked down at his drink. "I believe her name is Molly."

Henry felt himself tense at the mention of her name. Some men would call for a fight right there, for mentioning a decent woman's name in a place like this, but he let it pass in favor of getting further into the issue. "I believe it is, and I believe you opened your mouth to her in ways you had no call to."

O'Leary's eyes narrowed but he did not look at Henry. He just said, "Opinion."

Henry took a deep breath to try to steady himself. "Let me remind you of something. I never asked to go to your place. You asked me to, and then she asked me to."

O'Leary still looked straight ahead. "Fact."

"And no one asked you to come and talk to someone I might know."

O'Leary turned and smiled. "No harm done."

"What?"

"I said, no harm done. No more than you did."

Henry saw in that moment that O'Leary did not think anything illicit had gone on in his absence. He must have gotten some idea of what his wife had let out of the bag, and he was simply acting out of malice in return for Henry's having been a party to the knowledge. He was using the supposed offense as a cover. Henry decided to call him on it. "You did more than I did, and you know it. You had no business makin' the play you did."

O'Leary shrugged and looked back at his drink. "I thought them Indian girls was good for that. Give 'em a pair of red socks and—"

O'Leary did not get to finish his sentence. As soon as he mentioned Indian girls, Henry set down his beer. Then he moved his left foot forward and came across with his right fist, knocking O'Leary and his barstool to the floor.

O'Leary looked up from the floor and said, "I can see it's got you bothered."

"Shut your mouth, O'Leary. And if I hear about you openin' it again like that, I'll do worse." Henry looked around and saw several faces, some strange and some familiar, taking in the scene. Saying nothing more, he settled his hat on his head, turned around, and walked out.

It was night as he rode back to Ruby Canyon. Now he knew how McCloud must have felt, how tempting it must have been to put a boot in O'Leary's face. At least he had gotten in a punch, for better or for worse. For some onlookers it might have confirmed a suspicion that his errand to Crow Creek had not been innocent. But at the same time, he was clearly no longer under the shadow of a supposed friendship with Van O'Leary.

CHAPTER 10

IN THE CLEAR light of day, Henry imagined he wasn't done with O'Leary yet. The man was like some kind of insect he couldn't shake, the kind that clung to you and got its hooks into your flesh. He was like a tick that had to be pinched out just right, or it worked its way in deeper—or like a leech that if you pulled at it wrong, just got longer.

It was often easy to look back at a problem and see the point at which a person could have done things differently if he had known. Henry thought he might have avoided all this if he had declined going to town on that Saturday night back in May, or if he had cut the topic off sooner when O'Leary talked about branding slicks. He could have turned down the request to check on the Missus, or he could have let her letter go unanswered. In short, if he had been less of a friend to either of them, he wouldn't be in as deep as he was in the leech pond.

There did seem to be something perverse and deliberate about O'Leary. Henry thought that if he had been able to brush him off one way, he might have come back another way all the same. And now that O'Leary had been knocked off his stool, he was likely to find some new way to twist the truth around.

Henry did not see a good way to be sure he was shed of a man like O'Leary. Anyone as dishonest as he was would be likely to end up in the hoosegow. But if justice came anywhere near him, he would be the type to want to bring someone else down with him. Henry had heard that a raccoon knew how to drown a dog by putting all its weight on the dog's head and digging in, especially if it wasn't a large breed of dog. The old coon hunter O'Leary would have his version of that.

Before the sun had risen very high, Henry had brought out his tools and returned to work on the corral. Once he had the rails done, he could rig up a makeshift gate and not have to leave Beau on picket at night.

He had paused in his work for a moment when he heard horse hooves on dry ground behind him. He looked over his shoulder and saw Finch, riding a large gray horse he had undertaken to break for Cyrus's use.

Fifty yards out from the cabin, Finch waved as he stopped the horse. He held up his hand to let Henry know he needn't put down his hammer and come out. When his horse put his tail down, Finch dismounted. He took out a pair of leather hobbles from the saddlebag and hobbled the horse's front feet. Then he took off the bridle, sauntered into the yard, and hung the bridle on the hitching rail.

Finch's blue eyes swept across Henry's corral project. "You haven't got much done on this in the last six weeks."

Henry looked at him. "I can't seem to get a thing done."

Finch motioned with his head toward the horse. "Do him good to wait a little while." Then he stretched his neck as if to peek into the corral. "Shall we?"

Henry took advantage of the help when he had it. For all of Finch's meddling, he was a good worker, and if he offered to help, it wasn't for just a few minutes. The two men finished the rail Henry had been working on, ran the top rail after that, and nailed on a cap rail.

Finch took out his folded handkerchief, tipped back his hat, and wiped his brow. "See? You had enough lumber."

Henry looked at the pile that was left, which consisted mainly of warped and split planks he had discarded along the way. "Just barely."

He went to the cabin and brought out a pail of water and set it in front of Finch with the dipper handle pointing at the guest. As Finch dipped a drink, Henry said, "What news?"

Finch peered up from beneath his heavy eyebrows. "There was a fight in town last night."

"Is that right. So you rode out to tell me."

"Not really." Finch handed the dipper to Henry. "I got to town right after you left. Little buddy had just got back up onto his barstool."

"Good for him. I suppose he had plenty to say."

"Oh, you know him, the way he talks. Him and that coonskin English he likes to throw around. He got all het up and said, 'That kay-yo-tee better not come 'round lookin' fer trouble wid me. I kin shoot a squirrel's eye out if I'm close enough to see the squirrel.'"

Henry laughed at the imitation, which was credible. "I don't plan to go looking for him. I just hope he stays away from me."

"He does talk."

"Uh-huh." Henry gathered that Finch had come to report a little more and to trade it for what Henry might have to offer. So he asked, "What all did he say?"

"He said you didn't really have anything on him but you were letting on like you did, to keep his mouth shut about somethin' else."

"About what else?"

Finch flicked his eyebrows in his nonchalant way. "He didn't say, but he didn't really have to."

Henry's mind flashed a quick picture of Dora. *I have you to thank for some of that,* Henry thought. He set the dipper in the bucket and said, "So he accuses me in advance, of blackmail."

Finch shrugged. "Sort of comes out that way. I guess it depends on what you have on him."

Henry looked at Finch. That must be why he rode out, to get the rest of the story. Henry squinted and said, "Even if I had something on him, I wouldn't use it that way." He decided that was as much as he should say about either the branding or the bigamy. As for the other part Finch was fishing for—the reason Henry had wanted to shut O'Leary's mouth—Henry let it pass. O'Leary had apparently said nothing about Molly, and Henry did not want to bring her into Finch's understanding of affairs.

Finch shrugged again. "I doubt that people put much stock in what he says anyhow." Then he clapped Henry on the shoulder. "They said you landed a pretty good one. I'm glad someone did."

Henry gave a small frown. "For as much good as it did me."

They sat and made small talk for a little while longer, until Finch must have decided he had learned as much as he was going to learn. He took the bridle back out to the horse, which had been grazing all this time, slipped the bridle onto the horse's head, unbuckled the hobbles and put them away, mounted up, and waved good-bye. Then he touched spurs to the big horse and was gone in the direction of the Box Elder.

Henry kicked at a scrap of lumber. O'Leary had indeed twisted things, and there was no sense in going to town and hollering on the street corner to try to set the story right.

As he had reflected during the conversation with Finch, he had something on O'Leary—two things, for that matter, although the maverick proposition was just talk. The information about the bigamy really was something of substance, but it wasn't his place to bring it out. Yet if he said anything about either matter, he wouldn't achieve much in his own interest, and it would look like his charges were an act of petty revenge. It could even make it look as if he was trying to get closer to Mrs. O'Leary, which was an impression he did not want to give anyone. On the other hand, if he said nothing, he would seem to be confirming O'Leary's insinuation of blackmail. Henry shook his head. He really couldn't move one way or another; the best he could do was to say nothing and see what happened.

Henry had not expected to finish the bulk of the corral work so soon, and now that he saw where he was on lumber, he realized he would have to order more for the gate. He imagined he would not be able to have it delivered in time to use it before he went back to the Box Elder, but now that he had a little money once again, he thought it would be a good idea to put in the order. While he was at it, he could buy hinges and bolts. Then he could work on the discard pile and cut it into pieces for a feed bunk. Any useful pieces left over he could store in the dugout.

He wasn't eager to go back to town so soon, but he decided he would rather go on Friday than on Saturday, when there would be people in town for the weekend. With that plan, he spent the tail end of Thursday afternoon rigging up a gate out of rope and a cottonwood branch. He turned Beau into the corral and was done for the day.

That night he slept with the door open, as Beau did quite a bit of pacing when he first went into the corral. The horse had settled down by the time Henry went to bed, but at some point after midnight, Henry heard the horse whiffing and nickering. He slipped into his boots and went outside, called to the horse and settled him down, and went back to bed.

In the morning he saddled up and went to town, took care of his business quickly, and rode home. He was back by midday, so he decided to make some flapjacks.

When he went to put his hand on the bag of flour, he knew something was wrong. The flap was tucked to the right instead of the left. Whenever the flour got low enough for him to fold the loose end over, he always held the bag in his right hand, pressed the flap with his left, and set the flour on the shelf. He did the same with the coffee, rice, beans, and sugar. They all looked the same. He hadn't touched the rice, beans, or sugar since he had been back, and they still had dust on them. He had used the flour the evening before, to make biscuits, and he couldn't imagine having put it back on the shelf that way.

The only reasonable conclusion was that someone else had taken the flour down and put it back up. The only reason he could imagine was to lace it with another white powder. Of course an unknown visitor might have taken the bag down, done nothing to it, and put it back up on the shelf with the flap folded the other way. Maybe someone was looking for something he thought might be hidden in the flour, but what?

Regardless of whether the person was intending to poison him or not, he could take no chances. One thing was certain: someone had been in his house and there was no sign anyone had used the flour for cooking. He took down the bag of flour, carried it by the neck to the privy, and dropped it down the hole. It hit bottom with a solid thud. He was perturbed to think that even the cotton sack had to go, but he realized the evidence was still in one piece. Even though he would never retrieve the bag, it held the truth.

Back in the cabin he decided to boil all the rice, which would be enough for the next three meals. He started a fire in the pit outside, and while the firewood crackled, he went back into the dugout and pulled the rifle and its canvas sleeve out of the bundle of burlap. He set the rifle on his bunk, along the side of the bed next to the wall.

As the fire burned down, he crouched on his heels and shaped the bed of coals. He looked over at Beau in the corral, and he wondered if someone had been out there last night and had spooked the horse around midnight. It was difficult to find footprints on grass or on hard, dry ground. He saw none, just as he had found none in or around the cabin, yet he was sure someone had been there—at least earlier in the day if not during the night.

He poked at the coals. This was a rotten thing to happen, he thought. Up until now he had always lived free and open at Ruby Canyon, with no greater worry than the thought that his roof might leak in a big rain. Now he had to think about sleeping with a pistol under his pillow and a plank propped against the door. Or he could sleep like men did in the stories he had heard—out on the ground, with the horse's lead rope tied around his wrist. That was overdoing it, maybe, but he did need to remember he was on his own and quite a ways from anywhere.

In the morning he ate the last of the rice, noted the dust on the sugar and the beans, stashed the coffee in his bed, put the rifle back in the burlap bundle, and tied his pistol and holster to the saddle horn. Then he saddled Beau and headed back to town for a lock and chain. He thought about what he would buy. A common hasp might work all right in town, but out on the plains, a few blows with a chunk of firewood would take care of it. A bull-strong padlock and a heavy chain would provide more discouragement.

He had to try to think of everything. He couldn't assume O'Leary had made this move against him, but there was a good chance he was the one. And a fair chance he wasn't. Henry wasn't even sure whether it was a man or a woman.

As he rode to town, he was engulfed in sadness he at first did not understand. Then he realized he had lost something in this new turn of events. He had lost the freedom to go about his daily life without worry. Life had been open, without fear of his fellow man; now it was closed, tainted by suspicion. It was as if something had died, as if the bloom had gone and would not be back.

The sadness stayed with him, and he felt he could do himself some good if he talked to someone. Having to worry was bad enough, but having to feed on it alone would be worse. Although he had been planning to keep his distance for a while, he decided he would drop in on Molly, if only for a moment.

He bought the lock and chain at the blacksmith shop where he had bought the hinges. After that brief stop, he went to the mercantile.

Molly was just finishing with a lady from town when Henry pushed open the tinkling front door. He saw right away that she was wearing the sky-blue dress, and as she came down the aisle to meet him, he saw a pink ribbon in her hair. He wondered if she had a dress that color. He saw the darkness of her hair and the darkness of her eyes, and then he saw her face relax in a smile.

"Hello," he said.

"Hello."

"I was in town, so I thought I'd drop in."

"I'm glad you did."

"I didn't know how soon you'd want to see me again."

"Yesterday would have been all right." Her tan face had a glow to it.

"Really?" He felt a wave of gladness wash through him.

Her right hand brushed the dark hair back over her ear and behind her shoulder. "It's nice to see you."

The pink ribbon put him in mind of her little sisters. "Thanks," he said. "By the way, I didn't really get a chance to ask you the other day. How's your family?"

"Oh, fine."

"Have you gotten to see them?"

"Yes, they came into town in June."

"How are the little girls?"

A broad smile came to her face. "Just fine. Not so little, it looks like."

Henry smiled. "Be sure to tell them all hello the next time you see them."

"I will."

A brief silence followed. Henry found himself looking at the floor and then back up. Without quite meeting her eyes, he said, "I was wondering if you've heard anything else about me."

"I heard you took care of a bad medicine."

Now his eyes met hers, which were sparkling. "You heard, then."

"Oh, yes." She held up her hands. "But I didn't hear details. I just heard the skeleton of the story."

He gave a short laugh. "That's probably good enough." Then his mind skipped back and brought a detail forward. "I think I heard you say something."

She frowned. "What do you mean?"

"The thing you called him. You said, 'a bad medicine.' "

She laughed. "Oh, yes. That's what he his. He's a bad medicine."

"Wouldn't you say, 'He's bad medicine'?"

She cocked her head. "Oh, I see. People say it that way, but it's a little different the way I said it. A man like that is a bad medicine. If there was another one just like him, my father would call them two bad medicines."

Henry laughed again. It felt good to be laughing. "It sure fits him," he said.

There was another moment of silence until she spoke. "Well, how have you been, then? Are you back at the ranch?"

"Um, no. I've been back at my own place. And I'd say things aren't so well."

She frowned. "Really?"

He went on to tell her about the incident with the flour sack and the set of worries that came with it. She listened and nodded and frowned until he finished his account.

"That's not good," she said.

"No, it's not. Until I know who it is and get it settled, I can't live the way I ought to be able to. I have to keep a lock and chain on my door."

She put her hand on his arm. "Let's just hope you find out before long."

His eyes met hers, and he thought he could have kissed

her right then, until he remembered where he was. "Let's hope so," he said.

"Try not to let it worry you too much," she said, taking her hand away.

"Well, yes, I know. But if I'm not on my toes, something worse could happen."

"I know. But try not to let it devil you. I can tell it already has."

He looked at her. The clear features and the blue dress looked cool and reassuring. "Well, all right. I'll remember you told me."

"Yes. Do that."

Just then the bell tinkled on the door, and they looked at each other as the door opened.

"I'll be back before long," he said.

"Be careful."

"I will." He smiled. "If I can be careful without worrying."

She smiled and nodded as he turned and walked away. A stranger was coming into the store, a man in a light-tan broadcloth suit and a small-brimmed hat. Henry nodded to the man, who touched the brim of his hat. As Henry opened the door, he glanced over his shoulder and saw that the man had taken off his hat and was talking to Molly. Henry walked outside, gathered his horse, and left town.

As he rode home, he appreciated the way Molly had listened to his story and had seen its seriousness. Perhaps she hadn't seen it as thoroughly as he had, but that was natural, since she wasn't in his place. Perhaps also her encouragement not to worry too much was more easily said than done. But overall it had been an uplifting visit, even if it had been cut short. He remembered her hand on his arm, the comfort he had felt in just looking at her, and he remembered how her eyes had sparkled when she referred to what he had done to the bad medicine. She could be soft and spunky both. He smiled as he leaned forward and patted Beau's neck. "That's quite a girl back there," he said.

Henry was in bed with his pistol beneath the pillow and his rifle beside him when he heard hoofbeats. That was one thing about a dugout—it helped carry sounds, since the floor and walls were all a part of the ground outside. He pulled on his trousers and boots, slid the rifle out of its sleeve, and moved to the doorway. Now still in the dark he made no delay in getting into position. It was dark outside, and a man would have to come close to become a target.

The horse stopped about twenty yards out, just visible as a form, and a man's voice called out. "Henry!" It sounded like Charlie Dan.

"Who's there?"

"It's me. Charlie Dan."

"Come on in. Let me light a lantern."

Henry had a light going when Charlie Dan walked in. Henry was surprised to see his easygoing friend wearing a gun. "What's up?" he asked.

"I thought I should get out here with the news and not wait till morning."

"What news is that?"

"Van O'Leary has been found shot dead."

CHAPTER 11

HENRY BUILT THE coals of his firepit back into a fire and got a pot of coffee started. As he did so, he found out a few more details.

"Where did it happen?"

"Between his place and town."

"It must have happened pretty recently. I was in town earlier in the day, and I didn't hear anything then."

"It probably happened a little before dusk. His wife said he set out for town, and then when his horse came back, she got worried. She found him and came on into town."

"Were you there?"

"In town? Yes." Charlie Dan tapped his cheek. "My tooth got a little better, so I decided to ride in and see what was going on in town. Just to see the critter. I didn't stay long, of course. The news broke out at about ten, and I came right out here."

"I sure appreciate that." Henry looked at Charlie Dan in the firelight. "Do you know which horse he was riding?"

Charlie Dan shook his head. "No. Why?"

"Just wondering. I had the impression that the bay horse would go back to Windsor's on its own."

Charlie Dan smoothed the right corner of his mustache. "She rode a bay horse into town. Makes sense that if it came back with an empty saddle, she would have just gotten on him rather than take the trouble to saddle another one."

Henry tipped his head. "She wouldn't have saddled him as a first choice anyway. Maybe the bay's been at O'Leary's long enough that he thinks of it as home now." He glanced at the fire and back at Charlie Dan.

The two men went back inside to sit in the lantern light and wait for the coffee. Once inside, Henry thought to tell Charlie Dan about the apparent tampering with his flour. He covered the details carefully, using the shelf as an illustration, and went on to explain the related worries that the incident brought on.

As Charlie Dan listened, he pushed back his tan hat, rolled a neat cigarette, and lit it. At a pause in the commentary he said, "Why would he do something like that?"

"I don't even know if it was O'Leary, but that's my main guess." He felt a wince come to his face as he looked at Charlie Dan. "I suppose you heard about my little run-in with him."

"Of course. I heard it from Finch and then again in town."

Henry put his right index finger to his chin and glanced up at the shelf. "He's sure enough dead? Not just a rumor?"

Charlie Dan took a drag on his cigarette and said, as he exhaled, "He's dead, all right. The sheriff had a look at him before he sent for the wagon."

Henry took a deep breath. "I suppose I'll have some questions to answer."

Charlie Dan got ready to go back to town at daylight. Henry hadn't been able to sleep very well, but as he lay in the darkness it sounded as if his friend had gotten two or three hours of sleep. As Charlie Dan saddled up, he said, "Well, if no one bothers your place anymore, you can rest easy and figure it was O'Leary who messed with your flour."

"Uh-huh. But I'll still have to keep a lock and chain on my door for a while, at least, to be sure."

As Charlie Dan rode away, Henry thought the best thing

to do would be to stay put. If the unknown visitor had been someone other than O'Leary, that person would keep a distance if Henry was at home. Also, it would be a good idea not to be too hard to find if the sheriff came calling.

When Charlie Dan was gone, Henry decided he had better plan his eats for the rest of the day. Charlie Dan had helped him do away with the small flitch of bacon he had picked up in town the day before, and now he was down to beans. That was a long way from starving, but a pot of beans would also take nearly half a day to cook.

When he had the Dutch oven settled and smothered in the coals, Henry decided to take his rifle and see if he could scare up some meat. He hadn't seen any sage hens or wild turkeys near where he lived, but cottontails made their home up in Ruby Canyon a ways. He didn't usually care to eat rabbit in midsummer, because of the fever that rabbits were said to carry during bug season, but he planned to look it over carefully and cook it well. An alternative to eating rabbit was to drop a larger animal, but an antelope or deer would spoil in this weather, even in the coolness of the dugout, and Henry did not want to waste that much meat just to get himself a few meals.

He did not have to hunt long before he saw a rabbit sitting up in the shade of a clump of sagebrush. Henry thought of O'Leary shooting out the eye of a squirrel, and when he picked up the rabbit he counted himself lucky not to have taken off more of the shoulders than he did.

Henry was scooting the pieces of rabbit around in the skillet of bacon grease when he saw a buckboard being pulled by two horses. That would be the sheriff. Setting his fork on a rock by the edge of the fire, Henry rose to meet his visitor.

It was Gordon, all right. Henry recognized the short, heavyset figure who was balanced on the driver's seat. Around town, Henry had heard that the last horse Gordon had climbed onto had let out such a wheeze that the stable man had laughed out loud. A few years had passed since that story had gone into circulation, and Gordon hadn't gotten any lighter.

The sheriff brought the buckboard in at a slow walk and stopped it, tying the reins on the rail in front of the seat. Then the wagon tipped and creaked as the sheriff let himself down to the ground. He pulled his vest down, touched his flat-crowned hat, and started forward.

A few paces away, he held his right elbow out from his body and opened his hand for a handshake. As Henry took it, the sheriff smiled and said, "Good afternoon, Henry. I think it's noon by now, isn't it?"

Imagining that the sheriff's friendliness was just a preliminary gesture to warm him up for an interrogation, Henry answered, "I think so."

The sheriff glanced at the firepit. "Sorry if I'm interrupting your Sunday dinner."

"Not at all. You're welcome to join me, if you'd like your half of a rabbit."

The sheriff wrinkled his nose. "No, thanks. My wife will have dinner for me when I get back."

"Well, come on over while I tend to it."

The sheriff seated himself on a stump and sat with his legs apart and his hands on his knees. He cleared his throat as Henry squatted, but he waited to speak until Henry had turned all six pieces of rabbit.

"I don't know if you've heard about what happened last night."

"I heard something." Henry looked up from where he sat on his heels.

The sheriff's brown eyes were steady. "Van O'Leary was killed on his way into town."

Henry continued looking straight back. "That's what I heard."

The sheriff folded his arms across the swell of his vest but kept his eyes fixed on Henry. "Naturally, I have to look into it."

Henry nodded.

Something caught the sheriff's glance for a second, and then his gaze returned to Henry. "I understand you and O'Leary were friends for a while." The sheriff had apparently worked his way through the warm-up, as the tone of his voice had become harder and more characteristic of the man as Henry had known him.

"In a manner of speaking," Henry answered. "Not good friends."

"And I understand your friendship came to a pretty quick end." Then, with a flick of the eyebrows as if he didn't like to have to reveal his sources, the sheriff added, "That's the way it's told in the Gold Eagle."

Henry thought for a second. "It might seem that way, but I hadn't seen him for quite a while, and when I came back to town, I heard he had been spreading some rubbish about me."

The sheriff turned his head slightly but kept his eyes on Henry. "Would that have been his—er—suggestion that you were on friendly terms with his wife?"

Henry didn't like to see the case simplified, since it made it look as if he had simply punched a complaining husband, but he decided to leave Molly out of it for the present, so he said, "That's about it."

The sheriff's folded arms raised as he took a breath. "O'Leary was killed with a shotgun. At close range."

Henry winced. "That'll do it."

"I suppose a man of your caliber has firearms." The sheriff pointed his chin at the frying rabbit.

"Yes, but I don't have a shotgun. I had to shoot this fellow with my rifle." He stabbed the fork into a front quarter and held it up. "Took a big hunk off the shoulders."

The sheriff nodded, in the way that Henry thought a parent would nod at a child.

Henry shook the fork and let the piece of rabbit drop back into the skillet. "You can search my cabin if you want."

The sheriff still sat with his arms folded as he pushed

out his lips and shook his head. "I believe you." A couple of seconds later, he added, "Of course, from a practical view, if I had just used a shotgun that way, I wouldn't keep it around, either."

Henry felt his face tighten. "I haven't touched a shotgun in years."

The sheriff shrugged. "I'm just covering the obvious."

Henry gave the sheriff a hard look. "As far as what's obvious, I wasn't that friendly with his wife, either."

The sheriff flicked his eyebrows. "Why would he say you were, then?"

"I don't know. You might be able to find out something from her."

"From Mrs. O'Leary."

"Yes."

"I've already talked with her."

"Did she have any idea who did it?"

"She said she had no idea, that there might have been several individuals who disliked her husband."

"Did that include me?"

"She didn't mention your name, and neither did I." The sheriff glanced toward the corral and back at Henry. "Did you have anything on O'Leary?"

Henry felt his eyes narrow as he looked at the sheriff and said, "If I did, I wouldn't have had to kill him, would I?"

The sheriff pursed his lips. "No, it would probably be the other way around."

When Gordon had pulled himself back up onto the buckboard and driven away, Henry took the skillet of well-fried rabbit into the shade of the dugout. As he chewed the meat off the bones, he thought about the sheriff's visit. He didn't think the sheriff thought he was guilty, but that wouldn't matter much, especially in the public eye, until someone found out who had done the killing.

To look at it from the practical view, as the sheriff had said, Henry at least had to consider the dead man's wife as a possibility. She certainly had reason, especially if she had tried to leave and he had coerced her by some means to stay. As competent as she said she was with chores and heavy work, she could probably wield a shotgun. Furthermore, she was the sole reporter of the incident, so if she wanted, she could control the details that would then serve as a factual basis for an investigation. For as little as he knew her, Henry did not think she had done it, but he couldn't rule her out.

The strongest candidate, in Henry's mind, would have to be McCloud. The dark, moody rancher had cause, at least in some views, and he had shown he was capable of violence. Despite his disposition, McCloud did not impress Henry as a shotgun sort of man.

Finch could also figure in as a possible suspect. The man was always prying and snooping and sniffing. Henry had no idea whether Finch had any reason to pull the trigger, although he had shown an interest in O'Leary's wife. But in Henry's view, that made Finch an opportunist and not much more. Still, for all Henry knew, Finch could have been cutting out calves for O'Leary—but he doubted that, too. When it came right down to it, the main reason Henry could give himself for considering Finch at this point was that he didn't trust the man entirely.

Another possibility he thought he should entertain was Windsor. He may or may not have had reason, depending on the nature of work O'Leary was supposed to be doing for him. Henry broke a rabbit leg at the joint. The trouble with considering Windsor was that Henry didn't know enough about him or his dealings with O'Leary. Henry had the general impression that Windsor was a bit too dainty for the work—but then again, a firearm kept the job beyond arm's reach. A man didn't have to dirty his hands if he pulled the trigger. And then there was the odd underside to Windsor—

the strange laugh, the peculiar reflex of looking behind him. Henry nodded. He would keep Windsor in mind.

As for the unknown, Henry recognized that the killer could be someone he had never met—some person farther in the shadows. He recalled the sheriff's comment that Mrs. O'Leary had said there might be several individuals who disliked her husband. Henry imagined them scattered across the plains from here to Cheyenne, each standing in front of a cabin and holding a shotgun.

When he was finished with the rabbit, Henry tossed the bones into the firepit. Seeing that the coals had burned down more than halfway, he brushed the embers and ashes off the top of the Dutch oven so he could have a look. With a wooden pothook he lifted the lid, and with a wooden spoon he stirred the beans. They could stand to cook a while longer. He thought he might have just enough time to go see Cyrus Blaine and get back before the beans were burned.

Beau knew the way to the Box Elder, so he and Henry made good time. Henry found Cyrus at the big corral, looking over a crowd of cattle that had been sent to him from another roundup. Cyrus leaned against the corral with an elbow on one rail and a foot on the other as he listened to his hired man.

Henry didn't know how much Cyrus knew, but he started from the assumption that Cyrus knew nothing. That was the way Cyrus would have it. Henry put his boot on the rail and leaned his forearm on his knee. He told Cyrus a short version of the story of O'Leary and his wife; then he told how O'Leary had spoken lightly of a girl Henry knew, and had done so in the Gold Eagle, so Henry had found it necessary to clean his plow for him. Then the fellow had turned up dead, and naturally the sheriff had come to see him.

Cyrus's gray eyes were clear, and he followed the story with attention. He nodded at each major point, and at the end he said, "I had heard some of that already, but it's good to hear your side. I remember when he came into camp that day. He had some falling out with McCloud, didn't he?"

"Yes, he did. He was supposed to have sold some horses for McCloud."

"That's what I thought. I remember Perry got pretty worked up and then took it out on that rag-tail kid."

"Uh-huh. That happened right afterward."

"So now the jaybird is dead. You don't think McCloud did it, do you?"

"I don't know. But I know I didn't."

Cyrus smiled. "I'd've guessed that."

Henry hesitated as he looked down at his boot and then up. "Thanks."

Cyrus half-closed his eyes and nodded.

Henry took a breath. "What I'd like to ask for is a few days extra in case I don't get back in time. I don't want this to get in the way of my work, and I don't want to lose my place here."

"Don't worry about that. Take a few more days if you need 'em. If you're gone over a month, then maybe we should talk about whether I should take you off the payroll."

"I can't imagine takin' a month to get this straightened out."

"You do what you need to. Naturally, I can use the help as soon as you can get back."

"You're sure you don't mind?"

"I'm sure." Cyrus took his foot off the rail and stood up straight. "For one thing, you need to get the kinks out of your rope. And for another, it's just as well for me if this kind of trouble doesn't come onto the ranch."

Henry set down his own foot. For a moment he thought Cyrus was having second thoughts and might be thinking of letting him go. So he said, "But everything's all right."

Cyrus patted him on the shoulder. "Everything's all

right, boy. You go do what you need to do, and when you get everything straightened out, come back to your bunk at the Box Elder."

Henry felt his eyes moisten as he shook Cyrus's hand. He was shifting his weight to leave when Cyrus spoke again.

"But before you go, tell me one thing."

"What's that?"

"Is she pretty?"

Henry felt his face break into a smile. "You bet she is. I hope you get to see for yourself."

Cyrus half-closed his eyes again and smiled as he nodded. "Take care of yourself, Henry. And be careful."

"I will, Cyrus. And thanks."

Henry got back to the dugout at Ruby Canyon just as the sun was about to drop behind the rim. He turned Beau into the corral and checked on the beans, first noting that there was an even coat of ash over the top of the Dutch oven. The beans were cooked and had just begun to stick. He stirred them and sampled them. Good enough.

Then he went to unlock the cabin, and as he got up to the door, he saw a white piece of paper, folded up, tucked in between the lock and the two links of chain it was joining. He unfolded the paper and saw that it was an envelope with a letter inside.

Henry—

I imagine you have heard that Van has been killed. It has been more of a shock than I would have thought.

I hope you still consider me a friend. I feel that I need to speak with you about some of this, and I have thought that I might be able to help if you are having any difficulties.

With hopes that you will answer this note, if not in person, I am, as before,

Your friend,
Dora

Henry put the letter back in the envelope, refolded it, and put it in his pocket. It might do him a lot of good to talk to her. Then again, if he was seen coming or going, it could raise suspicion. He took out the letter and read it again. If anyone had a question about why he might go there, the letter gave a clear enough answer. He put the letter away again.

As he unlocked the cabin, he recalled what the paper had looked like, folded and wedged into the shackle of the padlock. He wondered whose hand had put it there.

CHAPTER 12

THE NEXT MORNING, Henry left for the homestead on Crow Creek before the sun had risen very high. The morning air was still cool, and Henry enjoyed the sounds made by the squeak of saddle leather and the jingle of the chain beneath Beau's chin interspersed with the occasional song of the meadowlark.

So far he had not felt much sadness for O'Leary, but now as he headed toward the dead man's place, he realized that all of these small pleasures of life had ended for that other person. Never again would O'Leary see or hear or feel any of it. The man was dead at a young age, and that was too bad. But Henry had little doubt that O'Leary had brought it upon himself and would not be missed greatly.

As he rode down into the yard of the little clapboard house, the place looked the same as before. It did not give him the feeling of emptiness he had felt in other places, where the spirit of the recent tenant seemed to linger. In those places, the hand of the deceased remained visible in the work he had left behind—just as Henry imagined his own hand would be evident in his dugout, his corral, his woodpile, and even his firepit. But here, he saw nothing that reflected the late owner. O'Leary had come to this country to make a new start, just as many men, himself included, had done. Some made it, some quit and went back, and some went on to the next place. Some died trying—and maybe that was a generous way to describe O'Leary.

Henry stopped in front of the house and called out to ask if anyone was home. Once again the door opened, and

Dora walked out. She was wearing a gray dress with thin black stripes running vertically—the closest thing, he imagined, to widow's weeds. Her mouse-colored hair caught the morning sun and looked clean, as always.

He dismounted and stepped in front of his horse. Dora gave him her hand and he took it, lightly, and released it. Her face looked drawn and worried, and the small mouth was pressed tight until she spoke.

"Thank you for coming."

"I got your letter, of course." He looked at her blue eyes, which had an anxious cast to them. "I didn't know who left it," he added.

"I did. But if I had known, I could have waited and asked your friend Mr. Finch to deliver it."

"Oh. I take it he's been by."

"To offer his condolences and his services." She bit her lip. "I'm sorry. That doesn't seem grateful enough. I think he probably means well with some of it."

Henry could not think of anything to say in response, so he said, "I was sorry to hear you had this trouble to go through."

"It's all right. I knew I was going to have trouble. I just didn't know it was going to be this kind."

"I don't know what I could do, but—"

"Some of it is already done. I've made arrangements, and the burial will be tomorrow morning."

Henry nodded. He had not thought he would go, and now he wondered if he should consider it.

"I don't expect many people," she went on, "and it's probably just as well."

He hesitated. "Well, if something comes to mind—"

"Actually," she said, looking down and then back up at him, "there is one thing. It's the main reason I wanted to talk to you."

"Go ahead."

Her eyes looked steadier than before as she opened her

mouth to take a breath. "What I told you about the marriage—"

"Yes?"

"I think it would be just as well if no one found out. That is, if you haven't mentioned it already. If you have—well, it can't be denied."

"I haven't mentioned it. I didn't think it was my part."

"Thank you. It would be a great favor to me if you didn't."

He shrugged. "That's fine with me."

"I'm not trying to protect him," she said. "But it's all so ugly. I feel the shame of it, even though I didn't do anything knowingly." She shook her head as she said, "I don't want any extra pity, either, because that would embarrass me even more." Her eyes looked pained but still steady as she looked at him.

Henry returned the look and nodded. "It's just as well left alone. You don't need to do anything about it now, so it doesn't need to come out."

"I'll write the other woman and tell her she doesn't have to do anything, either." Dora looked away. "She'll be free to marry again if she chooses."

Henry noticed her rough hands, folded together and resting against her stomach. "The same goes for you, I suppose."

She nodded, still looking away.

"You're young enough. You could meet someone else. Have a family."

She looked back, and her eyes had the anxious look again. "Yes, I could. I've already decided I'm going to go back to Ohio. I just have to sell the few things I wouldn't be taking."

"How about the place? The homestead."

She glanced away. "We didn't have much in it, and I expect to get even less back out of it."

Again, Henry didn't know what to say. He moved Beau's

reins to his right hand, and Dora must have thought he was getting ready to leave.

"Won't you stay a few minutes? I've got some coffee that's probably still warm."

Henry accepted, and within a few minutes they were seated, this time on the west side of the little house.

Dora held her cup and saucer on her lap. "Van's death hasn't caused you any kind of trouble, has it?"

"Yes, in the sense that the sheriff came out and told me I was under suspicion."

She winced. "Yes, he told me he was going to have a talk with you."

Henry felt a quick frown come to his face. "He said you didn't mention my name, and he didn't either."

She gave him a matter-of-fact look. "I didn't. But he did."

"Well, I guess he was bound to ask about me after what Van implied about you and me. I suppose you know about the fight we had the night before he was killed?"

"Only when the sheriff told me about it. At one point he even had the nerve to suggest that I might have done it—the killing, you know. Anyone could see I was upset, but he pressed right on with his insinuation."

Henry's eyebrows went up. "Well, as he would say, he was just covering the obvious."

Her cup clacked against the saucer. "Henry, I hated Van. Toward the end, I positively hated him. Sometimes I felt as if I could kill him, but I knew I couldn't. And I didn't."

"I didn't think so, but I wouldn't have blamed you if you had." Then he said, "Sorry. I didn't mean to be that blunt."

She took a deep breath as she stared at the ground in front of her. "No, that's all right. You don't know how much I despised him. I couldn't even stand to watch him eat. I would sit there and watch him, and it made me want to drive a knife into his hand." She blinked and looked up. "I'm sorry. I don't need to go on like that."

"Go ahead," he said. "I can listen."

"No," she said. "I've said enough. None of it matters anyway." She sniffed and rubbed her nose and went on to say, "I got us off the track. You were saying the sheriff has you under suspicion."

Henry sipped the lukewarm coffee. "Probably not without cause."

She gave him a close look.

"That little run-in I had with Van has the sheriff thinking that I had reason to go after him again, more seriously."

"Which you didn't, did you?"

"Of course not. But it looks bad for me."

"But I told the sheriff there was nothing to what Van said, that there was nothing between us. Didn't he believe either of us?"

"Hard to tell. He also asked me if I was holding any information on your husband."

"And you said?"

"I said that if I had anything to use against someone, there'd be no reason for me to kill him. He saw the truth in that, I guess, because he said, no, it would be the other way around."

Dora was silent for a moment and then said, "But you did have something."

"Well, yes, I did—two things, really. Besides what you told me about his earlier marriage, I knew Van made a little business proposition to me that he wouldn't want to become a topic of public conversation. It was only talk anyway, between him and me, so it wasn't much to hold against him. He invited me in on a venture to move a few calves, and I turned him down."

She said nothing, but the slight movement of her head told him it was familiar to some extent.

"So, I didn't think there was reason to mention either of those things to the sheriff, since I wasn't really holding either of them over Van anyway."

"Well, I thank you for not mentioning the first one. And the second one, like you say, was just talk."

"True. And it wouldn't make me look good, anyway. Now, as we're talking about it out loud like this, I've thought of a couple of things."

"What are those?"

"Did he have the goods on someone else?"

"You mean, did Van?"

"Right."

The eyebrows arched and the little mouth came together. "I couldn't tell you. He kept a lot of his business to himself."

"So I've gathered."

Dora shifted in her seat. "And what was the other thing you thought of?"

Henry took his hand off the coffee cup and looked at her. "What kind of work was he doing for Windsor?"

"Ranch work, I guess."

Henry felt the corners of his mouth go down. "That could include quite a few things."

"Well, I just can't tell you much about what went on between him and Mr. Windsor."

Henry paused, recalling the gossip and imagining Windsor on the street in Cheyenne. "I don't know what impression you've gotten, but from what I've heard, this fellow Windsor might not be on the up-and-up."

She shook her head. "I don't know."

Henry felt as if he had come up against a fence. "You don't seem to have much to say about him."

The small chin moved to one side and back. "To tell you the truth, Henry, I don't want to say anything carelessly until I find out if Mr. Windsor is going to buy this place."

Henry felt embarrassed. "Oh, I'm sorry. I didn't know there might be some business between the two of you." He looked at her, and seeing an apologetic look on her face, he added, "I'll just hang onto my questions until later."

She smiled. "Thank you. You're very kind." The smile broadened. "And I might know more by then, anyway."

Henry laughed and then, feeling relieved, went on to say, "I hope something works out in your favor."

The talk went on for a little longer. Dora did not ask about the chain and padlock on his cabin door, and he did not bring up the topic. The conversation came to a comfortable close, and Henry was back on the trail by mid-morning.

As he rode home, he thought about what a muck he had let himself be drawn through, and all to no purpose. Both of the O'Learys had brought him into confidences he hadn't asked for, and no good had come to anyone. It seemed like a waste of spirit, or a loss of small portions of his life, to be dragged into other people's schemes and problems and then to have to ignore what he knew.

If those issues had come to a dead end, he thought, then maybe he wouldn't have to worry much longer about the security of his own living place. But he knew he wasn't through it all yet. He thought he would let a few more days pass, and if no more strange occurrences took place, he might be able to return to a free and open life. Even more, he could hope that O'Leary's killer would become known.

Back at Ruby Canyon, Henry put Beau out on a picket so he could graze. He did not see evidence of anyone having visited, and that was good. After unlocking the cabin, he went about rustling up a bite to eat. He got a fire going outside, brought out the leftover beans to be reheated, and went to the spring for a pail of water.

While he was stirring the beans, he saw a rider in the distance. He watched the shape come closer, and he was not surprised to see Willis Finch on the large gray horse.

"Just in time for grub," Henry called out as Finch stepped down from the horse.

Finch looked at the sun as he tied the horse to the hitching rail. "You're a good man," he called back.

Henry continued stirring the beans to keep them from sticking. "Don't speak too soon. I haven't dished it up yet." As Finch walked toward the firepit, Henry asked, "Aren't you going to hobble him?"

Finch shook his head. "I can see you don't have any new work for me." He laughed. "I'll probably have to eat and run today."

Henry dished up two plates, and the men ate without talking. Each took a smaller second serving, and then chuck was over. At the moment when some men would bring out a pipe or the makings of a cigarette, Finch slipped his right hand into his inside vest pocket and withdrew two toothpicks. With the first two fingers of his hand, he extended a toothpick to Henry. Then he spoke.

"I guess I shouldn't have scared you so bad with that story about O'Leary bein' such a crack shot."

Henry drew his brows together. "What do you mean?"

"You got a big ol' heavy chain hangin' on your door post."

Finch could not see the doorway from where he sat, and Henry reflected that that was Finch's way—to take in a detail and then mention it later when the other person wouldn't expect it. Henry also wondered if Finch had seen it for the first time this afternoon.

Furthermore, he knew that Finch's comment was his way of fishing for an explanation. Henry decided to give him a brief one. "Just because two things happen one after another doesn't mean the first one caused the second."

"True." Finch smiled as he picked his teeth.

"For example, if you get food poisoning from the grub we just ate, you don't want to assume it was because I cooked it on an open fire."

Finch's quick blue eyes darted at Henry. "True. I'd assume it was because I didn't hobble my horse."

Henry laughed. Then he gave Finch the rest of the explanation he had planned to give. "Anyway, I put a chain on the door because I thought maybe somebody had been in my house."

"Really?"

Henry decided to bait a hook. If Finch could go fishing, he could, too. "Uh-huh. I made a batch of biscuits that just tasted like hell. Like a fool I ate half a dozen of 'em before I decided to throw 'em out."

Finch looked at him. "There's not a hell of a lot that can go wrong with biscuits. What did they taste like?"

"Sort of a metallic taste. Like when you fry an egg in a cast-iron skillet before you cured the skillet."

Finch made a face.

"Anyway, it made me think someone had been into my flour, so I tossed out the rest of it along with the biscuits. Then I got the chain and padlock."

Finch picked at his teeth for a few more seconds and said, "That's a hell of a thing to have to worry about." Then he gave Henry a serious look, knitting his brows above the quick eyes, and said, "Did they get into your coffee too?"

Henry laughed. "No. I'll make some."

A few drops of water slid down the outside of the coffee-pot and sizzled on the fire. After the silence had grown a while, Finch said, "I think it's funny you got such a heavy chain on your door, and such a flimsy gate on your corral. There's probably a joke in there somewhere."

Henry glanced at the corral. "I had to order more lumber. But you'll be happy to know I bought some very good hinges."

By and by the coffee came to a boil. Henry poured two cups, handed one to Finch, and sat down with the other. As he was taking the first sip of the hot coffee, he heard Finch say, "What do you think Windsor is up to?"

Henry held the cup steady and congratulated himself on not burning his tongue. "I don't know. Why?"

"He dropped in on the widow right after you left."

Henry looked sideways at Finch. "You don't miss much, do you?"

Finch's eyebrows went up as he laughed. "How would I know? Windsor probably thinks he doesn't miss much, either. He watched you leave."

Henry shook his head and looked at the coals. He appreciated Finch's tip, so he thought he would pay him back a little more. "From the little I was told, I gathered that Windsor might be dickerin' to buy that place from her."

Finch nodded. He usually seemed to know when he had gotten as much as he was going to get. He sat quietly as he finished his cup of coffee; then he stood up and shook out his cup in the old cow-camp habit. "Well, thanks for the grub, Henry. I hope it doesn't kill me."

"You're welcome. And I hope it doesn't kill either of us."

Henry walked over to the hitching rail as Finch untied the gray and tightened the cinch. It was then that he noticed the rifle and scabbard on the horse. If Finch was out snooping around, he was going prepared. Then in a second thought still prompted by the sight of the rifle, Henry remembered that Finch did not own a shotgun.

Finch walked the horse out a few yards, checked the cinch, and mounted up. He turned and waved, then touched spurs to the gray horse and moved out of the yard.

Henry watched Finch ride away. The man was a real bird dog, all right. Henry appreciated again the tip about Windsor. Then he recalled the conversation about the flour and the food poisoning, and he was convinced that Finch hadn't been the one to put a hand on his flour sack. Finch was just a free lance, maybe playing detective and maybe hoping to win a fair lady. Henry doubted that Finch had killed O'Leary. But until he knew who did, he couldn't be completely sure.

CHAPTER 13

WHEN HENRY WAS left to himself once again, he tried to relax. Other than running low on supplies and knowing he would have to go into town for more, he did not have much pressing him. The talk with Cyrus Blaine had put his mind at ease in that direction. Until the lumber arrived, he did not have a great deal of work around his own place. He could bring out his brace and bit, drill the holes, and mount the hinges on the part of the corral that was built, but as Finch would say, there was probably a joke in there somewhere.

He looked over the pile of split and warped lumber and decided he could work on that. It would give him the good feeling that the lumber wasn't getting any worse by lying in a loose pile in the sun, and he would have some firewood out of the scraps. So he got out his saw and went to work on it. By evening he had about half the pile converted into a mound of scraps and a neat stack of salvaged lumber.

That evening, as he fed some of the scraps into the fire, he estimated how much lumber he would need for a feed bunk. It looked as if he would have enough left over for a sawhorse, which would also work well for a saddle stand if he made it a little taller than a regular sawhorse. That idea appealed to him, as he could cut the pieces for the sawhorse as he went along and not have to recut from his good lumber later on. He did not mind the work, but every time he cut through a plank he cost himself some effort, and if he turned around and recut some pieces, he would be throwing out some of his own hard work.

The next morning, he went at his project under a cheerful morning sky. As he made his angled cuts, he took some humor in thinking that if he had a sawhorse, the work would go easier. Finally, by late morning, he did have a sawhorse. It pleased him to see such a useful apparatus standing on its own legs, having risen from the heap.

Now he had a sawhorse to work with, plus a surge of ambition to finish cleaning up the pile. He stopped only long enough to eat the last of the beans, and then he pushed on through. By early afternoon he had finished the salvage work and had also precut over half the pieces he would use for the feed bunk.

He rested in the shade of the dugout, in front of the open door and beneath the deer antlers. His arm and shoulder felt swollen, and his back was sore, but he had a real sense of accomplishment. As he got to thinking about a trip into town, he realized that O'Leary would be buried by now. Dora had said the burial would take place in the morning. Henry felt a tinge of remorse. He had been able to forget about that aspect all morning, and now the man was in the ground. Henry thought, if there was a good side to the way O'Leary ended up, it would be that he took a lot of trouble with him.

Henry washed, shaved, and made ready to go into town. A breeze lifted the saddle blanket as he was saddling the horse, so when he was finished with that chore he doused his fire. After a moment's consideration, he set the sawhorse inside the dugout. Then he ran the chain through the hole in the door and snapped the heavy padlock shut.

On his way to town he saw storm clouds up ahead. He reached back and felt for his slicker where it was rolled and tied behind the cantle of the saddle. He would be all right if it rained. Then he realized it might have been wise to have tucked his pistol in the saddlebag before he left. Finch and Charlie Dan were both going armed, and even if O'Leary was safely buried, trouble could still come around.

Although he knew it was possible, Henry couldn't picture sharing a common enemy with O'Leary. Even if it was McCloud who had killed O'Leary, Henry doubted that the dark lone wolf would carry it any further. McCloud might not know that the friendship had ended before O'Leary's career had closed out, but if McCloud had pulled the trigger on the red-haired swindler—which was how McCloud would have seen it—he would have been satisfied.

As Henry imagined Windsor, it took a little more of a stretch to make him into O'Leary's killer. But it was possible. He could even have led the bay horse and then sent it on into the yard so it wouldn't go back to his place. That was a thought. But then it was even harder to imagine Windsor having anything against Henry. Windsor knew who he was and had watched him leave the O'Leary place, but there was no logical reason for him to make a move against him.

Riding onward, Henry noticed that the storm clouds had moved to the east. He felt again for his slicker, and as he did so he thought once more that it would have been a good idea to have his six-gun along.

When he rode into town, water was standing in the main street, and people stood in small groups, talking, in front of the businesses. Then he noticed broken windows, and on the shady side of the street, in the gutter below the board sidewalk, he saw unmelted hailstones.

Henry patted Beau's neck. It gave him a queasy feeling to see the aftermath of a storm. Growing up in Kansas he had seen ugly storms, including tornadoes, and he knew that summer storms could carry incredible force. He was lucky, he thought, he and the horse both, not to have been caught in a hailstorm out on the open plains. But that was the way hailstorms were—they opened up over a relatively small area and then went away, leaving a battered mess to be cleaned up as the summer skies turned friendly again.

Back home he had once seen nearly the whole town beneath a three-inch carpet of leaves and twigs. Broad-leafed trees such as ash, elm, and cottonwood took it the worst, so a town that had been around long enough to have big trees could require enormous cleanup. It could also count on dead twigs and branches falling out for years to come. All of that came about, he thought, because of twenty minutes of fury that might just as well have dumped itself on the prairie if the weather pattern had been a little different.

Henry imagined that the cleanup of twigs and leaves would be minimal here, as Willow Creek did not yet have big trees. But little trees suffered, too, and the people who planted them would be disheartened. So would those people who had vegetable gardens.

Henry saw Molly right away. She was wearing a pale yellow dress and standing in front of the mercantile with Mr. Van der Linden. Henry recognized him at a distance because of his muttonchop whiskers. The man usually wore spectacles also; drawing near, Henry saw that they were in the proprietor's vest pocket. As Henry tied Beau to the hitch rack, Mr. Van der Linden moved down the sidewalk away from Molly. Henry stepped up onto the boards.

"Looks like you had a storm," he said to her.

Her face carried a strained look. "It was terrible. The hail was almost as big as chicken eggs." She made a circle with her right thumb and forefinger. "It was like sage hen eggs."

"How long ago was it?"

"A little over an hour ago. Most of it has melted by now." She glanced at the street and then back at him. "I tell you, Henry, it was scary. It sounded like a thousand men on top of the store, beating on the roof with hatchets." She pointed to the broken window on the left side of the door. "And this window broke with a horrible crash, like someone had thrown a rock through it."

Henry looked at the window. Jagged teeth on all four sides pointed toward the open middle. He winced. "How long did the storm last?"

"Barely fifteen minutes. But it broke windows all over town. They say there're windows broken on all four sides of some houses, and Mr. Van der Linden says it might be a month before we get enough glass in town to fix all the windows."

"What a shame." Henry glanced again at the broken window.

"We were lucky to be inside. Think of being out in the open—well, you were, but I'm guessing you weren't in it or you would have said so." Now she looked fully on him.

He met her look. "I was lucky. It missed me entirely. But I'm sorry to see such a waste of things here in town."

"Yes, it's terrible, isn't it?"

They went into the store, the safe interior that held the staples of flour, coffee, sugar, and the like, in addition to the other necessities of clothing, ammunition, laundry bluing, and strychnine. Henry made his purchases and offered to walk Molly home from work. She said she could visit with him for that long, but she thought that once she got home, Mrs. Sullivan would need her help at cleaning up from the storm.

After he left the mercantile, Henry went to the butcher shop and bought a chunk of salt pork. With still a little time on his hands, he checked on his lumber order, which should arrive, he learned, "as soon as next week."

With his packages in the corner of the barbershop and his horse still tied to the hitch rack, Henry was ready to walk Molly the few blocks that lay between work and home. Although it was a short walk, he was happy for the opportunity. Among other things, it told him she didn't mind being seen with him.

He had not talked to her since before O'Leary's death, and he had not formed an impression as to whether the public eye viewed him with suspicion. The merchants he came in contact with—Van der Linden included, for his brief moment—had given him no real sign. Business was business, and he imagined that few shopkeepers would reveal a prejudice on the basis of rumor—even if they believed it. And because the most vocal slights to his character had come from the dubious source of O'Leary himself, he thought he would be able to weather it out. Now that he thought of it, even Van der Linden's walking away could be taken as a good sign. A proprietor who harbored mistrust might have stepped in to shield the young woman, and her willingness to let him walk her home was an even better sign.

"I'm assuming you're still out at your own place," she said.

The shapes of his packages came to his mind. "Yes, I am."

"Have you had any more . . . trouble?"

"No, I haven't. I'm hoping I've seen the last of it, of course, but it might take a few more days for me to feel easy." Henry thought of O'Leary, and he imagined a new grave that had already been there long enough to be pocked by hailstones.

"Let's hope so," she said. "I've thought about it several times since you told me, and it seems so—ugly, to know that someone has been through your personal belongings."

"Like a rat in the pantry. But whoever my rat was, he's not going to gnaw through a lock and chain."

"That's good. But it's too bad you have to lock your place."

"I probably won't always have to." He looked at her. "I'm hoping things get better, you know."

She smiled. "I hope so, too."

At the Sullivans' house he touched her hand, met her eyes, tipped his hat, and turned away. He looked back once, and she had already gone into the house.

On the ride home, Henry watched the skies and the landscape. The world was calm, stretching away in all directions with not a detail out of harmony with the broad picture. The range land lay quiet. Here and there he would see a handful of cattle, and once he spotted a band of antelope. Occasionally a large bird swooped down to the grass and back up. White clouds lay above the horizon to the south, but off to the west, where the sudden storms usually came from, the sun was slipping down in a cloudless sky. As he neared the end of his ride and dusk came on, he heard the strange honk of the nighthawks, or bullbats as he had heard them called. He looked up and saw two of them floating on the air currents in the dimming sky.

As he rode across the corner of his homestead and up to his yard, the cabin and corral lay in shadow. Beau snorted and tried to turn away, but Henry headed him in. Coming closer to the cabin, he saw an object hanging in front of his door. It looked like an animal.

Closer now, he saw it was the body of a young coyote, a little more than half grown. It dangled on a length of heavy twine. Henry saw that the hemp had been tied around the base of the antlers that were nailed into the cross-beam above the door, and the other end of the twine disappeared from sight as it snugged under the neck fur of the coyote pup.

Henry unloaded and unsaddled the horse, leaving the tack and supplies by the firepit. Things weren't right, and dark was coming on; he told himself he needed to keep thinking clearly. He decided to picket Beau until bedtime so that the horse could eat, and he wished he had a solid gate for the corral. He had the lock and chain, but to put that around one end of a rope gate was just the stuff of one of Finch's jokes.

Before dark came on completely, he searched the ground in front of the dugout. He found the hoofprints of an unshod horse, but that told him nothing. Most of the horses in this grass country went unshod, unless they went to work on rocky ground or up in the mountains. As nearly as he could tell, there had been one horse, and the visitor must have carried the dead coyote in a burlap bag, as Henry could not find any drag or skid marks on the ground.

By now, night had come almost all the way in. Henry unlocked the cabin and pushed the door open. Holding in his stomach and brushing his back and shoulders against the doorjamb, he edged inside. He found the lantern and lit it, then moved to the hanging carcass and had a look. He could not see where a bullet had gone in or come out, and not until he looked over the head of the animal did he decide that it had been killed with a shotgun. It looked as if the ear had been torn by several pellets, and the short fur around the eye had a few pits that were now caked with dried blood.

Henry nodded. It would be nearly impossible to get close enough to an untrapped adult coyote to kill it with a shotgun. But a young one, if a fellow knew where the den was and then put out some bait—that could be done.

He kept his distance from the animal. Young or old, it was likely to carry ticks or fleas, especially in the summer. He didn't want to brush up against it, and he didn't want to cut it down and let it flop in the doorway of his living quarters. He held the lantern back inside the cabin, and his eyes lighted on the sawhorse. That would work.

Turning the sawhorse on its side, he walked it around the doorjamb and outside, where he set it up on its legs. By the light of the lantern from inside the dugout, he climbed onto the sawhorse, got a firm grip on the twine, and cut it free from the antlers.

The sudden drop nearly pulled him off the sawhorse, but he caught himself with the hand that held the knife. He steadied himself, stepped down from the sawhorse, and carried the pup into the darkness. Fifty yards from the cabin he let it onto the ground, and after that he dragged it nearly another quarter mile out onto the plains.

Back at the dugout he stripped off his shirt, checked himself for vermin, and washed himself thoroughly. The musky smell of the dog still hung in his nostrils, and he had little interest in eating. He put out the light and sat outside for a while, leaving Beau to graze a little longer.

As he sat in the dark, trying to make sense of this development, it seemed as if O'Leary was back at work. To overcome that uneasy notion, Henry told himself the man was dead and in the ground. This was someone else's work—someone who used a shotgun, and possibly someone who had heard or heard of O'Leary calling him a coyote. Of course O'Leary was dead and buried, and even if he had killed this pup, he would have put a bullet through it. So would Finch, for that matter. On Henry's short list of suspects, that left McCloud and Windsor—and, of course, a space for the unknown.

There was still no way to be sure, but as Henry sat there, he formed the conclusion that the person who had entered his cabin before was the same person who had hung up the coyote—which meant someone other than O'Leary—probably the person who had killed him. And if there had been any doubt that someone had handled the bag of flour to begin with, that doubt was gone. Someone was stalking him, taking a deadly game into his quarters and letting him know about it.

He thought again of the dark form of the coyote looming in his doorway. There was so much of O'Leary in the image, as if he had come back to haunt his acquaintance. Henry told himself again that the man was dead, but the sense persisted. Sitting in the dark, Henry had the gut feeling that regardless of who had made this move, the problem ultimately came from O'Leary. The trouble hadn't ended with his death but had lingered on. Henry hadn't asked for it, but he had let a sordid element into his life, and now it had come to his door. Whoever had hung the animal had to be perverse and malicious, and although Henry couldn't know the exact intention, the person was having some success at getting under his skin.

Sleep would not come easily tonight, that was for sure. Henry sat in the dark until nearly midnight, slapping mosquitoes and reviewing over and over again the image of the coyote hanging in the doorway.

Thinking that the maneuver might have been calculated to make him barricade his door, he could not decide whether to leave his door open or closed. He remembered stories about the old scouts, who liked to sleep in the midst of dry leaves and twigs so that no one could come near without sounding an alarm. Henry thought, as foolish as it seemed, he could strew the smallest thicknesses of firewood and brush kindling in front of the door. Then he could sleep with the door open, with an ear tuned for anything at the corral.

Still not sleepy, he spent a while laying out the twigs and sticks. He tried one step, and the noise sounded loud in the night. Even someone who tried to clear a pathway would make noise.

He led Beau to the corral and took off the halter. He thought of picketing the horse close to the door, but he decided not to leave the horse tied up for someone else's hands.

For the next two or three hours he tossed and turned. He slapped mosquitoes against his ear, got up twice to drink water. Not very much longer, he thought, and the first gray streaks would show in the east.

He awoke with a start. Morning light was pouring in through the open doorway. He pulled on his trousers and boots, slipped into his shirt, clapped on his hat, and tramped across the mat of twigs and sticks.

The ropes of the corral gate were lying on the ground where they had been cut and dropped, and the corral was empty.

Someone had come to Ruby Canyon, perhaps had waited outside the cabin to hear his even breathing, and had taken his horse. Now he was on foot—a long walk from anywhere, and in the open all the way.

CHAPTER 14

AS HENRY SLIPPED his holster and six-gun onto his belt, he imagined the walk ahead. He had decided to go to a homestead that lay about five miles due north, where he would ask to borrow a horse. From there, town and the Box Elder lay at about equal distances. In either place he could borrow a horse for a few days. Then he could return the homesteader's horse, provided that he could borrow it to begin with. From there he could return to Ruby Canyon and try to pick up a trail. The few tracks he had been able to find were headed south.

Henry buckled the belt. A rifle would give a man much more assurance than a six-gun, but a homesteader might not welcome the sight. After that, a rifle could prove awkward if there wasn't a scabbard handy to go along with whatever horse and saddle he might borrow. Henry tried to think of anything good about being on foot with only a six-gun. He shrugged. He would be able to see someone coming at quite a distance, and a man with a shotgun would have to come within pistol range.

Of course, he couldn't depend upon this unknown person having only a shotgun. Someone had killed O'Leary with a shotgun, and someone—probably the same person—had killed the coyote with a shotgun also. But that didn't mean the person didn't have a rifle or know how to use one. The shotgun could be something of a disguise—for someone like Finch, for example, who was devious enough to think of such a thing.

For all of Finch's caginess, Henry did not think he had

killed O'Leary. Because Finch had obviously been kept out of a compromising situation with Dora, Henry couldn't imagine him having enough cause, and Finch's casual contempt for O'Leary expressed more detachment than a killer would likely have. As he thought back on it, Henry realized that Finch had not even mentioned O'Leary's death during his last visit. Henry was even more certain that someone other than Finch had stolen the horse. Finch was a horseman, and the code of the range ran deep in him. He might bird-dog a coon hunter's wife, but he wouldn't take a fellow cowpuncher's horse. Still, Henry told himself he had to keep Finch in mind.

The tracks led south, in the direction of both Windsor's and McCloud's places. As Henry thought of the dark rancher, he could imagine the man's brooding anger taking the shape of violence. But McCloud would not have stolen the horse; like Finch, he was a horseman and a man who went by the code. He had cuffed that kid Fred for laying a hand on another man's horse, and even if he felt justified in an act as extreme as killing O'Leary, and even if he still extended his grudge toward Henry, he would not have stolen the horse.

As for Windsor, Henry could imagine him as possibly having a reason to shoot O'Leary, but he could not come up with an explanation of why Windsor might hang a dead coyote on his door or steal his horse—or possibly poison his flour.

Henry went to the doorway and looked toward the south, trying to make sense of things. He knew he couldn't even be sure the thief had come from or gone to the south; a clever person could just have created that impression.

Henry had checked the six-gun before he put the holster onto his belt, and now he checked it again to make sure he had the hammer on an empty cylinder. "Five beans in the wheel," he had once heard the old sheepherder Manders say. Henry slid the pistol back into the holster. It never hurt to check a firearm a second time, especially when a man had a lot of other things going through his head.

He stood at the doorway and looked out. The country stretched away empty as far as he could see. He gave the cabin a once-around look, closed the door, chained it, and snapped the padlock shut. A few yards from the cabin, he looked back and saw the woodpile where he had restacked the twigs and small branches. His glance went to the corral, where the rope gate lay on the ground. Then he turned around and started his walk.

The sun had climbed nearly halfway up in the morning sky when Henry came to the homesteader's fence. He walked along the fence until he came to a corner brace, then followed the fence around the corner for about a quarter mile until he came to a gate. A small dwelling made of rough lumber sat about forty yards in from the gate.

Henry called out, "Anybody home?" He watched the front door, but it did not move. Then a movement at his right caught his eye, and a man appeared from behind the corner of the shanty. He held a rifle pointed at the ground.

"Good morning," Henry said, waving with his right hand and then resting the hand on the gatepost where the man could see it.

"Mornin'." The man's hat brim shaded his face. "What kin I do for ya?"

"My name's Henry Sommers. I've got a homestead a few miles to the south. I was wonderin' if I might talk to you for a minute."

"What about?"

"I've lost my horse. Turned up missing in the middle of the night. I was hoping I might be able to borrow one."

"For workin' yer place? Or for how long?"

"Just long enough to go get some help. I think I might have some tracking to do, and I can get another horse to do that."

"Come on in."

Henry crawled through the wire strands of the gate and walked toward the house. The other man leaned his rifle against the doorjamb and waited in front of the doorway.

Henry held out his hand. "Pleased to meet you."

"Likewise." The man put out his hand. "What did you say your name was?"

"Henry Sommers. I've got a place south of here."

The man nodded. "Name's Bressler."

Henry expected the man to say more, but he didn't. Henry went on to say, "I work at the Box Elder, over to the north and west of here. If I can make it over there, I can get mounted well enough and go look for my horse."

Bressler's glance took in Henry's gun and then returned to make eye contact. "Big outfit?"

"Not very big."

"You takin' up land so you kin turn it over to them?"

"Nope. It's my own place, and I hope to keep it that way."

Henry could see the man's face now. He imagined Bressler to be his age or younger. The face had a smooth texture, still uncreased except at the corners of the eyes. Bressler's hair was a light brown, and on the sides of his head between the ears and the hat brim, the hair was cut short and running to an early gray.

"I've got but two horses myself," Bressler said. "I could let you have one, but I'd like him back as soon as you could git him to me."

"I can do that. And I sure appreciate it."

The horse looked like a granger's horse well enough. It had a lean and rangy build, plus a long tail and cracked hooves, but the sorrel coat was shiny. Bressler put a halter on the horse and led him out of the corral.

"His name's Spencer. If you've rode them ranch horses, I don't think he'll give you any trouble."

Henry took the lead rope and patted the horse, which

stood still with his head down and forward. "I'm sure he'll be fine."

As Henry rode away from the Bressler place, he looked at the sun. He figured he could keep from pushing the horse too hard and still arrive at the Box Elder when the men were in for dinner. He had not seen a rider all the time he was walking, and he felt even less likely to be bothered now that he was riding the red horse.

The men were still eating when Henry walked into the bunkhouse, so Henry sat down and joined in. One by one, the others left the table and went to the next room. When Henry finished eating, he went to his bunk.

Finch was stretched out in his usual manner, with his hands behind his head and a toothpick in his mouth. Charlie Dan and Andy were seated by the open doorway, smoking, and Andy had the buggy whip for swatting flies. Henry knew that they would all have seen the different horse he was riding, and he wondered who would make the first comment.

Andy said, "Didn't expect to see you so soon."

"Something came up," Henry said back.

Charlie Dan glanced out the doorway, in the direction of the place where Henry had left the horse. "Finch said it looked like you'd been in a poker game."

Finch spoke up. "I said it by way of a compliment. I said Henry wouldn't ride a crowbait like that one out of choice."

Henry looked at Finch and then at the other two. "No," he said, "I had to borrow that horse." All three men were looking at him, and even Finch, who often put on a poker face, looked curious. "I lost mine," Henry added.

"He didn't just run off, did he?" asked Charlie Dan.

"Not from the looks of it. Someone took him out of my corral last night—or early this morning. I had a temporary gate, and someone cut the ropes." Henry nodded toward Finch. "The one you joshed me about, day before yesterday."

Finch widened his eyes. "I guess it's serious."

"I sure think so." Henry looked around. "I'd like to see if I could borrow that black horse, Rocket, and go out on a search."

Finch said, "You ought to have someone go with you."

"I don't like to ask. I don't even like bringing this much trouble onto the ranch, but I do need a horse."

"Cyrus went to Cheyenne," Finch said. "It's all right with me if you take a horse." He glanced toward the doorway. "What do you think, Charlie Dan?"

"I'll go along."

Finch shifted the toothpick with his tongue. "If you don't stay gone more than a couple of days, there shouldn't be a problem."

Charlie Dan nodded and dropped the last of his cigarette onto the floor. He ground it out with the sole of his boot and scooted the debris out the doorway.

Andy looked at Henry and said, "Pistol-packin' weather, ain't it?"

Henry and Charlie Dan made good time on fresh horses. As they rode, Henry told about the visit with Dora, without mention of the bigamy, and then he told about the dead coyote. He also repeated what Finch had told him about Windsor watching him. He did not mention any uncertainties he had about Finch, but he did bring in McCloud long enough to say that he didn't think McCloud would take a horse.

Charlie Dan agreed. "But this other business. The dead coyote and the flour before that. Whoever did those things, he seems a little off-center to me."

The dark shape of the coyote came to Henry's mind. "Seems that way to me, too."

When they got to Bressler's place, Henry noticed clothes drying on a clothesline in back of the house. Bressler came out the front door and met them at the gate. After Henry had handed back the horse and had thanked Bressler for the loan, the other man shifted his jaw and spit on the ground.

"Somethin' I didn't think to mention earlier."

"Oh? What's that?"

"I saw a little outfit headin' south of here yesterday."

"Really?"

Bressler nodded. "Two men, and a little bunch of horses. I'd say about a dozen head."

"Headed south?"

"I'd say. I saw 'em over west of here about this time of day, but I didn't go up close and ask questions."

Henry nodded. A man didn't ask questions of strangers unless he had good reason. "Were they moving fast?"

Bressler turned down the corners of his mouth. "Faster'n a herd of sheep, but not as fast as a man by himself."

Henry thanked him for the information and again for the loan of the horse. Then he held out a little cloth bag of raisins he had gotten from Hollis. "Here's a little something that your wife might like."

Bressler took the bag. "Don't have a wife. But thanks."

Henry and Charlie Dan decided to follow Bressler's tip rather than go back to the cabin and try to pick up a trail there. They moved faster now, angling to the south and west until they found the tracks of a horse herd. The trail was easy to follow, so they continued at a running walk. After a little while, Henry could tell that the horses had taken the trail west of his place, where the mantle of the earth rose gradually to form the northern rim and western end of Ruby Canyon. Anyone following this trail would have swung wide of Henry's place, as was now evident to Henry and Charlie Dan. They kept an eye out for tracks leading from the main trail back to Henry's corral, and even though they saw none, they continued on their first hunch. They agreed that the horse herders, on their own or paid by someone else, might have absorbed the brown horse into their own herd. Henry and Charlie Dan followed the trail past the canyon and found where the other men had camped on Sage Creek, at a spot that Henry estimated was a couple of miles upstream from Molly's folks.

Henry looked up at the sky. "They're over half a day ahead of us."

"I'd say," said Charlie Dan. "But if they're not runnin' fast, like as not they took a good rest at noontime to let the horses graze, and they'll be lookin' for an evenin' camp before long."

Henry nodded. "If they're not runnin', they probably don't have Beau. But it's our one lead, and we've got to check it. I wonder if we could catch 'em by dark."

Charlie Dan looked up at the sky. "Hard to say. But we'll sure gain on 'em."

They moved on, following the trail as easily as before. Ever so slightly it veered back toward the east, but it still ran in a predominantly southern direction, toward Cheyenne.

As late afternoon was slipping into early evening, they came to a creek where they rested and watered the horses.

"Do you think we've come to Bear Creek yet?" Henry asked.

Charlie Dan laughed. "I don't know. We could ask Finch."

Back on the horses and pushing forward, they traveled another eight or nine miles. A row of treetops told them there was a creek ahead, and as they topped the last rise of ground they saw a horse camp in the creek bottom. There was just enough daylight to make out the camp and the horses at that distance.

Riding in slowly, Henry counted fifteen horses and got a better look at them. Half a dozen of them were picketed and the rest were hobbled, and not one of them was Beau. At the campsite, a man moved to a heap of saddles and packs and stepped back with a rifle in his hands.

"Hello the camp," Charlie Dan called out.

"Come on in," said a voice.

Henry and Charlie Dan dismounted and led their horses into the camp. Dusk was coming on darker by the minute now, so that the fire cast its own light outward.

Two men stood on the other side of the fire. Henry thought they might be brothers, as they looked alike. They were of average height, both slender, wearing loose-fitting clothes without vests or bandanas. Each man wore a hat with a brim that curled up on the sides and a crown that had a narrow crease on top. Both men had long brown hair tucked behind the ears, and their stubbled faces took on a shadowed look in the firelight. The men were probably in their late twenties, and the roughness seemed to have settled firmly into their appearance. Henry noticed that each man had a gun and holster on the right, and a sheath knife on the left. The man with the rifle had it pointed down toward the fire, in a pose that was neither menacing nor friendly.

"Evenin'," said Henry.

"Evenin'," came the answer.

"Sorry to trouble you."

"No trouble." The man with the rifle was doing the talking.

"Name's Henry Sommers. This is my friend, Charlie Dan Logan. We ride for the Box Elder, up north of here."

"Almost to the end of your range, aren't you?"

"A good part of this is still open. But we're not chasin' cattle right now, anyway. We're lookin' for a lost horse."

The man without the rifle spoke, in a deeper voice than his partner's. "You won't find him here."

"I can see that."

"We got papers on all of these," the deep voice answered.

"I don't question it," Henry said. "But you can understand why we wanted to ride in and have a look."

"Not a problem."

Henry glanced at Charlie Dan and then back across the fire. "I suppose we'll be movin' along, then. Sorry for any bother."

"No bother at all," said the first man, the one with the rifle. "You're welcome to stay." He lowered the rifle so that it pointed at the ground by his side.

"We've got a few more miles to make," Henry said. "But thanks all the same." Henry motioned his head at Charlie Dan.

The deep voice came back. "Well, good luck. I hope you find your horse."

"Thanks. And good luck to you, too."

Henry and Charlie Dan mounted up and crossed the creek, then turned upstream. They let the horses move to the higher ground and find their way. After a couple of miles, they turned back down to the creek and made camp. In a little while they had the horses picketed and a fire blazing.

"Well, that turned into a lost cause," Henry said. "Ride all day, just to run into that rough pair."

Charlie Dan poked at the fire. "Sure came to a dead end," he said. "But you can't blame Bressler."

"I don't blame him, but he could have told me earlier instead of waiting till I brought his horse back."

"Well, if he got any kind of look at them, it would've been a good guess to say they were horse thieves." Charlie Dan gave a half-smile.

"From the looks. But they did say they had papers on all of 'em."

"Probably do, if they say so. It's sure not our place to ask." Charlie Dan stroked his mustache, yellow in the fire-light.

"Nope," said Henry. "That's up to someone else."

After a moment of silence, Charlie Dan said, "You know, Henry, that seems like the kind of outfit where you could expect to find that kid Fred."

Henry nodded. "Isn't that the truth?"

The next morning, Henry and Charlie Dan decided to cut back east and head toward home through Windsor's part of the country. They ate canned peaches for breakfast, then used the cans to boil coffee. The men took their time, giving the horses another half hour to graze. Then as the sun was starting to climb in the sky, they saddled the horses and moved out.

Charlie Dan said he had a vague notion of where Windsor's place was. While they didn't have any right to question Windsor, Henry thought they could at least pay a visit and tell the new-money man what their mission was. They could keep their eyes open along the way, and if nothing else, they would be back at the Box Elder by late afternoon or early evening.

At midday, when they were within what Charlie Dan estimated to be a few miles of Windsor's place, they saw a rider coming from the east. They decided to head straight toward the rider, who might be able to give them directions and might even know something about a lost horse. Once they set a deliberate course toward the other rider, the distance between them diminished until Henry could guess at the identity of the dark rider on the dark horse.

"Looks like McCloud."

"It sure does," said Charlie Dan. "Or his brother."

When they were within waving distance, the parties waved back and forth. A few minutes later, they were within speaking distance.

"Good afternoon," Henry called out.

"Same to you."

It was Perry McCloud, sure enough. Henry saw him giving them both a good looking over, no doubt taking in their ropes and their six-guns.

Charlie Dan spoke up. "Warmin' up, isn't it?"

McCloud just nodded, and after a brief silence he asked, "You boys findin' any Box Elder cattle down this way?"

Henry took that to mean a different question, which he answered. "We're lookin' for a lost horse. Mine. Someone took him out of my corral, night before last."

McCloud's right hand, which had been out of view, came up and smoothed down the large mustache. Without looking at Henry, he said, "That's what this country's comin' to."

Henry said, "It was that brown horse of mine. You know him."

Now McCloud looked straight at him. "Boy, I don't know a damned thing. That friend of yours beats me out of not one but two horses, and then he goes and gets himself killed. All I know is I'm left with nothin'." He shook his head. "I used to think I knew how this country worked, but now I don't think I know a thing. Except this. You have anything to do with someone like that, and you deserve to come up empty-handed. That's what I tell myself. It was some of it my own fault." He looked straight at Henry again. "There might be something in that for you."

Henry nodded. There was no use arguing. He could see that McCloud thought Henry was responsible in some way, that he deserved to lose his own horse if he had been friends with a swindler.

Charlie Dan spoke again. "Well, we're still lookin'. We thought we'd drop in on that new fella Windsor and ask him if he's seen anything."

McCloud looked at Charlie Dan. "He's not home. I just came from there."

"Oh."

"You can go on over and see for yourself. But he's not there."

Charlie Dan looked at Henry. "No sense in going out of our way."

Henry twisted the corner of his mouth and nodded.

McCloud turned to the off side, hawked, and spit. Then he turned back and looked at Henry. "Time was, when a man owned something, he owned it. And if another man took something, he made him pay." McCloud wrinkled his nose, and the mustache twitched. "Now you don't know who to look for."

"Uh-huh."

"Makes a man damn good and mad when he doesn't get to make someone pay. But that's the way it seems to be nowadays. That's why I say I don't know a damn thing." McCloud touched his hand to his hat. "I'd best be movin'. Say hello to Cyrus."

The young men said, "So long," and watched McCloud ride away. When he was out of range, Henry said, "Well, that made everything clear, didn't it?"

"Like mud."

"Looks like we came to another dead end."

Charlie Dan pushed his tan hat back about an inch. "Uh-huh."

"Do you think he went to Windsor to try to collect some money, or to talk business?"

"What kind of business?"

"I don't know. Like I was telling you yesterday, Windsor might be getting his hands on the O'Leary place. Could be that McCloud is trying to squeeze out something that way, or he could be trying to collect on any wages that Windsor might owe O'Leary."

Charlie Dan squinted. "It's hard to tell. It sure looks like Windsor has a hand in it somewhere, though."

"I think so, too. I keep comin' back to him as I think it all over, but he doesn't seem like the type to pack around a dead coyote or wait up all night to steal a horse."

"You never know."

"That's for sure," Henry said, as they put their horses into motion. "And he could have paid someone to do it."

Henry gave a short laugh. "Except he's probably close on money."

Charlie Dan turned in the saddle. "Didn't you say that Mrs. what's-her-name might have more to tell?"

"Yes, I did."

Charlie Dan looked straight at Henry as the horses jogged along. "Maybe you need to go talk to her again, to find out anything else there is to find out."

Henry felt himself frown. "I think you might be right. As much as I don't like the idea, I think that might be what I should do."

CHAPTER 15

HAVING DECIDED TO pay Dora another visit, Henry did not return to the Box Elder with Charlie Dan. They parted ways on the upper ground at the west end of Ruby Canyon, where Charlie Dan went on north to the ranch as Henry dropped down to the east to return to his cabin. He spent about half an hour trying to pick up a trail that the horse thief might have left, but he could find nothing definite. Until he had an idea of where to look, a horse in this big country would be about as easy to find as a button that dropped into the sea of grass. Thinking that a visit with Dora might lead him to a better plan, he headed back for his cabin.

Nothing seemed out of order when he got there, and he could not find any sign of new visitors since he had left the morning before. The sight of the cut ropes on the corral gate brought up a raw feeling again, and although the coyote had left no marks on the door or threshold, he still had a strong memory of its physical presence. He had killed coyotes himself and skinned them as well, so he wasn't squeamish. But the idea of a dead one hanging on his door was repugnant, and he wondered if any ticks or fleas had dropped to the ground at the entry of his living quarters.

Unsure of the best way to secure the black horse, Henry tied it to the hitching rail for the time being. He unlocked the cabin and went inside, where among a few odd pieces of tack he found a bell. It was an item he had saved from his night-wrangling days, many years earlier. On roundup, the leader of each string of horses had a bell, each with a different tone. The nighthawk learned all the different tones, and as he rode around the horse herd at night, the bells would help tell him if any animals were straying. Henry had been a night wrangler for only one season, but he had ended up with a bell and had kept it. Until now, he had never had a use for it.

He thought first of tying the bell around the neck of the black horse but on further thought decided against it. A person waiting in the night would know he would have to quiet the bell. It might be better to rig up the gate again and tie the bell to one of the ropes. That way, the bell would not be tinkling off and on throughout the night, but if someone tampered with the gate, it would sound. Pleased with the idea, Henry picketed the horse to let it graze until bedtime. With some loose pieces of twine, he put the gate back together and tied on the bell.

The sun went down, casting cool, pretty shadows on the corral and cabin. From sleeping out on the trail the night before, Henry knew that the moon was down to a sliver and would not shed much light. So when darkness had settled in and the campfire had burned down, Henry carried his bedroll to the north side of the corral. He brought in the horse and closed the gate. Then with his rifle by his side he stretched out on his bedroll in the darkness, where he could hear the sounds of the horse in the corral.

No unusual noises came in the night. Henry awoke from time to time, listened for the horse, and went back to sleep. At daybreak he awoke again, this time to the cool stillness of morning, when the growing light mixed with the smell of dust and grass and sagebrush and horse. He lay still for a few minutes, heard the snuffle of the horse and the first tink-a-link of the meadowlark. Then he rolled out.

After picketing the horse to graze once again, he untied the bell and put it back in the cabin. He built up the fire and went about fixing coffee and flapjacks for breakfast. He checked the salt pork and thought he would use up some of it, also. By the time he had finished his morning meal, cleaned up, and shaved, he had decided to go see Molly before he went to talk to Dora.

The sun had climbed to its midmorning elevation when Henry and Rocket came to the edge of town. Life seemed to be going on as normal, with the exception that some windows were boarded up. Henry turned onto the main street and rode to the mercantile, where he tied Rocket to the hitch rack. As he stepped up to the sidewalk, he noticed that Mr. Van der Linden had gotten the window fixed.

The bell tinkled as Henry walked in. He saw Molly at the counter and waved. She waved back. Seeing no other customers in the store, he walked directly to the counter. She was wearing the lavender dress he had seen before, and her hair hung loose behind her shoulders. His eyes were adjusted to the indoors by now, and he liked the shades of color from her hair to her face to her dress.

"Hello, Henry." Her dark eyes sparkled as she said it.

"Good morning, Molly. How do you find yourself today?"

"Just fine. And you?"

"Well enough." He paused, comfortable with the moment but unsure of what he really wanted to say. He had wanted to see her more than he had planned anything in particular to talk about.

She looked past him, in the direction of the window. Raising her eyebrows and smiling, she said, "Is that your new medicine dog?"

He turned and saw Rocket, already dozing at the hitch rack. "Huh?"

"Don't you usually ride a brown horse when you come to town?"

"Oh. Um, yes, I do." He looked at her. "This is one of the ranch horses. I'm riding him because someone took my brown horse."

Her face turned serious. "Really?"

He nodded. "You remember what I told you about having to lock up my cabin?"

"Yes. You thought someone might have laced your flour."

"Right." He took a breath. "Well, when I got back from town the other day, I found a dead coyote hanging on my door."

Molly flinched, and her face clouded.

Henry went on. "Naturally, I think it all has something to do with O'Leary, but I don't know how."

Her eyes looked troubled as she said, "You've got to be careful, Henry. Whoever it is, isn't right in the head." She pointed to her own skull.

"You're the second person who said as much. I just need to find out who he is before he makes another move."

Her eyes seemed to be searching his face. "I hope you can," she said.

Henry put his hands palms up on the counter, and she put her fingers on his. He looked around, and in a lowered voice he asked, "Is Mr. Van der Linden in back?"

She shook her head.

Still in a low voice, he said, "I think it might be that new fellow, Windsor, but I don't know what his angle is. There's a person who might be able to tell me something." He looked her in the eye, and he felt his face tighten as he said, "Mrs. O'Leary."

Molly gave him a steady look. "Then you should try to find out."

Henry felt his eyes start to water. "That's what I thought. I wasn't sure how easily I could tell you, but I wanted to see you before I went out there."

She smiled. "I'm glad you did."

"Thanks. So am I." He pursed his lips and then said, "I don't know if she's in on it with him or if he's trying to take advantage of her, but I think she's in a position to know something." He pressed against her fingers, and she pressed back.

"Be careful," she said.

"I will. And thanks."

As Henry rode toward the little homestead house, he wondered if this would be his last visit with Dora. He hoped so, for her sake; she had said she planned to go back to Ohio, and he wished her well. He thought about the timing of his visit. He knew there was a possibility that she had some level of confidence with Windsor, so his own coming by unexpectedly would lessen the chance of crossing paths with Windsor—unless the man was already there.

The house looked forlorn as always, and to Henry's relief he saw no horses tied to the hitching rail. When he was within a hundred yards of the house, he saw movement on the shady west side, and he realized Dora had been standing in the shade, watching him approach. He waved and she waved back.

Henry tied the black horse to the hitching rail as Dora came forward to meet him. She looked drawn and anxious, as usual. She was wearing the light-colored print dress with a sunbonnet, so he imagined she had been outside when she saw him coming.

She seemed to pay no attention to the horse. Squinting in the bright daylight, she said, "I wasn't expecting you."

Henry took her hand and released it. "Sorry to drop in on you unexpectedly, but I was hoping you wouldn't mind."

"Not at all." Her eyes roved, looking at him and the sky beyond and back at him. "I haven't any coffee made."

"Please don't bother," he said. "I don't expect to stay long."

"Let me bring out some chairs. There isn't much shade right now, but the little bit of breeze feels good."

When they were seated, Henry began by saying, "A couple of things have happened since I saw you last, and I thought that if I told you about them, you might be able to help me puzzle it out."

She gave him a questioning look.

Henry scratched the side of his head. "A little while back, just before, um, your husband died, I thought someone had been in my cabin and had tampered with my food. So I bought a chain and padlock to put on the door. After he died something else happened. Three days ago, I went home to find a dead coyote hanging on my front door." He paused and saw an uncomfortable look on her face, and his glance flickered to take in her hand against her stomach. He went on. "The next morning, my horse was gone." Motioning with his head toward Rocket, he said, "So I borrowed this horse from the ranch where I work, and I'm out trying to put things together."

Dora shook her head. "That's awful." Then she looked straight at him. "Who would do such things?"

Henry's eyebrows went up and down. "I don't know—at least, I'm not sure. I thought you might know something else that would help me."

"Like what?"

Henry hesitated. "The last time I was here, you said you might be able to tell me more about Mr. Windsor."

She looked down.

"I don't mean to be pushing," he said, "and I don't want to ruffle things if you're still trying to sell this place to him, but the time has come for me to try to find out as much as I can."

She shook her head and looked up. "I was wrong about him. He wasn't planning to buy this place."

"Oh." Henry waited for her to go on.

"He says Van owed him money."

"So he expects you just to turn the place over to him?"

"He knows I want to leave, and he says it would be the fair thing to do."

"Quite the gentleman."

She glanced at Henry and then gazed at her hands, which were folded on her lap. "At first he was very nice. He said he would like to acquire the place, but when I suggested a cash settlement, he really changed."

Henry said, "He may not have all that much money to spare."

Dora looked at him. "It wasn't very much money to speak of."

Henry thought for a moment. He couldn't come right out and ask how much O'Leary supposedly owed Windsor, or why, but if he could come to that information, it might be useful. After a long moment of silence, he asked, "Could you tell me what kind of dealings Windsor had with your husband?"

Dora hesitated and then said, "As I told you before, I didn't know much in detail."

Henry shrugged. "Just about anything might help."

Dora looked at her hands and then back at Henry. "I think Van might have spoken to you about buying and selling calves."

Henry gave a quick thought to the offer O'Leary had made. The man had offered money, and he might well have given his wife a softer version of the scheme. She seemed to know that the plan had not been entirely on the square, but she was describing it in those terms. Henry said, "That's a way of putting it, but yes, he mentioned it."

"Well, Mr. Windsor was going to be what you might call a silent partner. He was supposed to know someone he could sell to. And he put up some money for Van to buy calves."

Or pay someone to supply them, Henry thought. Then his mind went back further for a second. Windsor and O'Leary had both stayed on at the Gold Eagle that first night, and O'Leary had laid out the maverick proposition the next day. "Was this about the time Windsor sold him the bay horse?"

Dora blinked her eyes and after a couple of seconds said, "Yes."

"So, Van was supposed to go out and acquire some calves?"

"Yes, and they were going to sell them, and Mr. Windsor was supposed to get his money right back."

"Hmmm. Did he round up any calves?"

"Not that I know of, but I think he led Mr. Windsor to believe he had them."

Henry considered for a moment. "What about his business trip? He couldn't have had any calves by then."

Dora turned down the corners of her mouth. "That was supposed to be a little horse-trading trip, to raise money."

"Uh-huh. He took a couple of horses belonging to a man named McCloud."

"Yes, and one of Mr. Windsor's, and who knows what else."

Henry frowned. "What did he do with all the money?"

Dora paused, cocked her head, and said, "Giving money to Van was like pouring water down a gopher hole. No amount ever made a difference, and no one ever knew where it went."

"Do you know whether Windsor ever asked Van for some of the money back?"

Dora nodded.

Henry could see it—O'Leary putting up a stone wall just as he had done with McCloud. "So he told Windsor he didn't have it?"

"That," she said, "and I think he might have done a little worse."

"Oh?"

"I think he might have suggested to Mr. Windsor that the silent partnership could become . . . not so silent."

"Blackmail?"

She pushed her lower lip against her upper lip and nodded.

Henry let out a low whistle. That could very well be the reason O'Leary got shot out of his saddle. But there were still a couple of loose ends. One was McCloud. Why had he been on his way back from Windsor's? "Tell me," he said, "do you know if Windsor was ever in cahoots with a man by the name of McCloud?"

Dora frowned. "Not that I know of."

Then it occurred to Henry that if Windsor had not been at home for McCloud's visit the day before, he might have come to see Mrs. O'Leary. He asked, "When was the last time you talked to Mr. Windsor?"

"Yesterday." She was looking at her hands again.

"And that's when you found out there wouldn't be a cash settlement?"

She looked at Henry, and he could read resentment in her eyes. "Yes," she said. "That's when he changed."

Henry hesitated. "Is there anyone else you might be able to sell it to?"

Her spirits seemed to pick up as she smiled. "Mr. Finch has offered, but I turned him down."

Henry laughed. The bird dog has missed his point again.

"This place was proved up on when we bought it," she went on, "so I have the deed free and clear. I don't have to give it away. I can go back to Ohio, and sooner or later I'll get an offer I can accept." She looked at Henry. "I'll be leaving in a few days. I can sell a few little things, including the horse, and be on my way."

"Just one horse?"

"Mr. Windsor took back the other one. Like you said, he's quite the gentleman."

"I should say so." Henry thought for a few seconds and then said, "That still leaves me with one question."

"And what would that be?"

"Someone has been stalking me, like I told you, and I've got a strong feeling it's Windsor."

Dora gave him an open look. "It could be."

"If it is, my question is, why?"

Dora took a breath. "He probably thinks you know some of these things I told you."

"About the silent partnership." Henry recalled the scene in the Gold Eagle, when Windsor saw him with O'Leary.

"Yes. And he might even think you got paid for some calves. I truly don't know what Van told him."

"If he thinks I was working with Van, he must think I'm in a position to blackmail him too. Maybe he even thinks I owe him money if I was in cahoots with Van." Henry thought of Beau and the cut ropes.

"That could be."

Now the image of the dead coyote came to mind. "Dora," he said, "do you know anything else about Windsor?"

"In what way?"

"Whoever hung that coyote on my door has got to have some mean spirit in him."

"I don't know," she said.

Henry shrugged. "That's all right. What you've told me gives me plenty to go on."

She looked at him. "You got dragged into all of this just by being a friend, didn't you? A friend of Van's and then a friend to me. I'm sorry. Very sorry."

"I wouldn't say it was your fault. I think I could have managed things a little better myself, but I'm not exactly sure where. Anyway, that part's in the past, and I'm not kickin' about it. Right now, you're being a friend by telling me what you can."

"Thank you," she said. "I'm glad to know I'm doing some good, after all."

Henry hesitated, then spoke. "Would you be willing to tell some of these same things to the sheriff?"

She pursed her lips, then relaxed them. "Yes, I will."

"Would it be all right if I dropped a hint to the sheriff and suggest he pay you a visit?"

She nodded, then looked at Henry. "Yes. It seems like

the least I could do at this point." She gave him her hand. "Thank you for being my friend, Henry. I don't know if I always deserved it."

Henry took her hand, gave it a light squeeze, and released it. It did not feel as rough as it looked. "Thank you, Dora. You've stood by me. I'll remember that."

As Henry got ready to leave, he noticed that the sun was directly overhead. Rocket was standing on his own shadow. Henry took the horse to the trough and watered him, tightened the cinch, swung on, and rode past Dora, who stood in front of the house.

"So long, Dora. And good luck," he said, touching his hat.

"The same to you, Henry."

A little ways out, he turned and saw her still standing in the sunlight. He waved, and she waved back.

CHAPTER 16

HENRY TOOK THE long way home, swinging by town so he could drop in at the sheriff's office. As he rode, he reviewed the conversation he had had with Dora. He concluded that she must have gotten some of her information from Windsor himself. He was convinced that there had been some degree of confidence between Dora and Windsor. Apparently she had waited to tell tales on him, but she did. That told Henry she had changed her mind about Windsor. For his own sake Henry knew he was lucky that Dora and Windsor had had a falling out. Otherwise, she might not have given him the information that was helping him make sense of what had gone on. Regardless of the nature of her dealings with Windsor, she had helped him and he was grateful.

Once in town, Henry went straight to the sheriff's office. Gordon remained seated at his desk, with his hat on, as Henry walked in. He had his arms folded across his vest, and he lifted his right hand to indicate a seat for his visitor. The brown eyes stayed focused on Henry all through the interview, as Henry told about his missing horse and then explained what he had heard from Mrs. O'Leary. Henry concluded with the suggestion that the sheriff go out to speak with her.

"I have some idea of how to conduct an investigation," the sheriff said. "I've already spoken with Mrs. O'Leary, as you know, and I've already spoken with Windsor."

Henry felt a rush of anger come on, but a warning came with it and he was able to hold it back. "What I'm trying to suggest is that there's new information to be collected."

The sheriff screwed his mouth to one side and then back. "You don't know how much information I collected before."

Henry met the gaze of the brown eyes. He was pretty sure the sheriff simply didn't want to concede that some-one else might know more than he did. So he said, "Yes, sir, that's true. But I think we both know more now than we did before about who was blackmailing who."

The sheriff's gaze flickered. "What we actually know and what you heard may not be the same."

Henry's jaw tightened and released. "I came here first because I thought I should. But if you're just going to sit here—"

The sheriff raised his eyebrows and tilted his head back about an inch, all the while keeping his arms on the crest of his stomach. "I was on my way out when you came in. So don't worry about whether I'm just going to sit here. Meanwhile, the best thing you can do is go home, stay put, and keep quiet. If I need you, I'll either send for you or come and get you. Let me handle this. I don't need anyone interferin' with my investigations."

Henry stood up. "There's still the matter of my stolen horse."

"You've made me aware of that," said the sheriff, looking up and nodding. He held the brown eyes steady on Henry. "And if you go home and stay put, I'll know where to find you if I need you."

Henry walked outside and untied the black horse. He was sure that the sheriff would eventually act on the new developments, but Gordon's attitude still rankled him. Absorbed in thought, Henry turned the black horse into the street, mounted up, adjusted his reins, and moved forward. As he looked ahead, he felt a jolt in the pit of his stomach. Coming straight toward him, dressed in the clean suit and hat as always, was Windsor on horseback.

Henry's first impulse was to try to avoid Windsor. But

that might arouse suspicion, so he rode ahead without moving his reins.

Windsor continued straight on. Soon they were face to face, just the two of them in the street.

Henry stopped the black horse. "Good afternoon," he said.

Windsor stopped his own horse, the one he had been riding when Henry had met him that evening on the prairie. "Good afternoon," he answered, touching the light-colored hat.

Henry took a breath, waiting for the other man to speak again.

"Sorry to hear about your friend," Windsor said, almost quickly, as if to fill the empty space.

Henry looked at him. The blue-gray eyes were steady, and the face looked calm. The left hand holding the reins was resting on the saddle horn, and the right hand was out of view. Henry met his gaze. "It was too bad," he said. "We weren't such good friends by that time, but it was too bad all the same."

"It must be hard on his wife," Windsor answered. "Do you know how she's taking it?"

Henry's thoughts raced. Of course Windsor knew Henry had seen her; Finch said Windsor had watched him leave. And Dora told him she saw Windsor just yesterday. "I've seen her," said Henry, "and she seems to be holding up all right."

"I'm glad to hear it." The blue-gray eyes held steady. "And everything's fine with you, I hope."

"Just like always," Henry said. "Work and more work."

Windsor nodded, and the Vandyke moved as he said, "Good enough." He raised his left hand from the saddle horn as if to move his horse forward.

"By the way, Mr. Windsor."

The left hand settled on the horn, and the eyes flickered for an instant. "Yes?"

"I've lost a horse. The brown horse I was riding the last time we met. You haven't seen him out your way, have you?"

Windsor turned down his mouth and shook his head. "No, not at all."

"Well, I'd appreciate it if you'd keep an eye out for him. He's a good horse, and I'd hate to lose him."

"I certainly will." Windsor gave him an earnest look. "If I find a stray horse, I'll leave word here in town."

"A brown one."

Windsor gave a firm nod. "Yes, indeed."

Henry touched his hat. "Appreciate it. And it's been good seein' you."

The other man's right hand came up to return the gesture as he said, "My pleasure." Then both horses moved, and the meeting was over.

Henry felt the tension flow from him as he rode out of town. He didn't know why Windsor had come to town, but there was no reason to think he had been following Henry. He had apparently been taken by surprise when Henry appeared on the black horse, but he had managed the small talk with good composure. Henry licked his lips and realized his mouth was dry. The short meeting had not told him much, except that Windsor had all the poise of a well-practiced liar.

Henry rode back to Ruby Canyon in the hottest part of the afternoon. He saw no signs of anyone having been around the cabin or corral, so he unsaddled Rocket and relaxed for a few minutes. The horse had worked up a sweat, and when he had cooled down and dried off, Henry watered him and then picketed him out to graze.

Henry sat in the shade against the face of the dugout. Now all he could do was wait. He was pretty sure Windsor was a step behind and did not know how much cause there was for alarm, so it was a matter of letting the sheriff take his time doing his work. Henry scratched in the dirt with a twig, telling himself he shouldn't resent the sheriff so much. Then he remembered what the sheriff had looked like as he lowered himself from the buckboard and later as he heaved himself back in. At least there was something to smile at, and the sheriff was not incompetent. He was going to do things his way, but he would probably get something done.

Although Henry didn't like being left to cool his heels this way, he felt he had been able to take more control of the problem than he had before. Going to see Dora had been a big step in taking the problem back to its source and meeting it on its own terms. That course of action had taken him closer to getting things resolved than the search for the missing horse had. And although he had to stay put for the time being, he didn't feel hobbled.

Henry drummed his fingers on his knee. It was the waiting that ate on him as much as anything—the waiting and the idleness. He wished he could get things settled and go back to work. Today was Friday. The sheriff might make it out to see Mrs. O'Leary by this evening, but he probably wouldn't come by Ruby Canyon or look up Windsor until tomorrow. Henry decided that if the sheriff didn't have results by Monday, he would ride out to Windsor's himself and then go back to the Box Elder. Cyrus would be back from Cheyenne, and Henry could try to settle into a normal course of work.

That evening he tied the bell back onto the gate, and when the night had turned dark he took his bedroll outside. It was a warm night, and Henry stayed awake slapping mosquitoes until after midnight.

Daybreak came on clear and peaceful. Rocket was looking out across the top of the corral, but as Henry followed his gaze he could see nothing that might disturb the calmness of the morning. Henry rolled out of his bed, got dressed, picketed the horse to graze once again, and went about his morning tasks.

After breakfast he brought out his tools and laid out the leftover lumber. Building the feed bunk would help pass the time, what with all the cuts he would have to make and all of the detailed work of fitting and nailing. Also, it would give him the good feeling that he was getting something done while he waited.

Finally he had the bunk complete and standing on its own four feet. He took a long moment to admire it, this solid piece of work that might last him for years. There was no telling how many horses would ever eat out of it. Henry looked at Rocket and then off to the south, wondering where Beau was. It wouldn't be easy for a man to sell a branded horse without a bill of sale, and Henry could put out the word for other riders to be on the lookout. He shook his head. It was hard to imagine that the horse was gone, just like that—but then again, sometimes it was hard to imagine O'Leary on his back in a dark box, never to rise and make trouble again.

Henry gathered up his tools and put them inside the cabin, along with the sawhorse. Next came the feed bunk. As long as a coffin and twice as heavy, it was too cumbersome for one man to pick up and carry, so Henry lifted it one end at a time and walked it into the corral.

By now the sun was straight up. The feed bunk stood on its own shadow, as did Rocket. Henry went into the cool of the dugout to rest a while. He lay on his back, looking at the shelf and the bundles hanging from the ceiling. He closed his eyes.

He awoke with a start. He swung his feet onto the floor, stood up, grabbed his hat from the table, and went to the doorway. Then he relaxed as he saw Rocket swishing his tail and grazing.

Henry stretched and yawned. It was about time to move the horse, anyway. He walked out into the warm, bright day. The world was still, and the only motion he saw was the swishing of Rocket's tail. When he got to the horse, he saw that a horsefly was making a bother. With each swish of the tail and shiver of the horse's hide, the large black-and-gray fly would rise and then light again. Henry stood by the horse's shoulder and raised his hand, and as the horse flinched, Henry slapped the horsefly. The huge bug flipped to the ground, where it lay on its back, thrashing its legs and fluttering its wings. Henry brought the sole of his boot down on the fly, pressed and twisted, and dragged his foot against the grass to clean the sole. He patted Rocket on the neck and said, "Out of business." Then he pulled the picket pin and moved the horse.

The shadows were starting to move off of dead center when Henry saw a speck in the north. He stood up from his campsite to watch, and as the speck grew, it looked like a buckboard. It seemed to widen and narrow, until Henry realized there was a horse and rider alongside the wagon.

The figures came on slowly, merging and separating. The party went through a low spot, so that Henry could see only dark tops. Then the tops rose out of the ground and became figures again, still moving toward Henry's place at Ruby Canyon.

The buckboard turned to one side and then back, as a team and driver might do to avoid a badger hole. Then the wagon straightened out and came closer. When the party was less than half a mile away, Henry began identifying the individuals. First he recognized the rotund figure of the sheriff, who belonged with the buckboard. Then he turned his gaze to the rider, and he recognized the posture. It was Willis Finch, on a dark brown horse that Henry recognized as a Box Elder mount.

The little party covered the ground that lay between Rocket and the cabin. The black horse watched and nickered as the group went by. Finch waved, trotted his horse out ahead of the buckboard, and pulled in at the dugout. He swung down, tied his horse to the hitching rail, and turned a beaming face toward Henry.

"Ready to ride?"

Henry looked at the sheriff, who was bringing the buckboard to a stop in a small cloud of dust.

"Go ahead and saddle up," Gordon said. "We're on our way out to Windsor's."

Finch watered the two buckboard horses and his own as Henry saddled Rocket. Before long, the group was continuing south across the plains.

Henry supposed he had been invited along on account of his missing horse. He was not sure why Finch was there, but he imagined he was on horseback so that the sheriff would have room for a passenger on the return trip. Finch rode out ahead of the wagon, which Henry took as an invitation. When they were well ahead, Henry looked across at Finch. "Are you being a helper?"

Finch looked back. "I found your horse."

Henry smiled. "You did?"

Finch nodded in his matter-of-fact way. "When Charlie Dan came back, I thought I might go out and do a little lookin' around on my own. I found out where Windsor had your horse holed up, and I beat it back to the sheriff. I knew we had the evidence then."

Henry said, "That's great!" Although Finch wasn't beaming, Henry could see he was taking pleasure in getting set to pull the rug out from under Windsor.

Finch reached inside his vest and took out a clean toothpick. "Meanwhile, of course, the sheriff had been out to talk to Mrs. O'Leary. She told him about all the dealin's between Carrot Top and Mr. New Money. About like she told you, I guess." Finch shifted the toothpick in his mouth. "So, between the horse and what the missus said, the sheriff has plenty of cause to haul him in."

Henry glanced back at the sheriff, who had not shown any eagerness to speak to him. He looked back at Finch, who gave a tight smile and nodded.

* * *

Windsor's ranch headquarters consisted of a drab little house facing south. Across from the house stood a barn and corral, the latter engulfed in weeds. As the party rode in from the west side, Henry could see that the barn door was open, as was the front door of the house. The sheriff tied the reins to the rail in front of his seat, then let himself onto the ground and pulled his vest down to his waist. Henry and Finch dismounted and tied their horses to the hitching rail.

"Wait outside," said the sheriff. Then with his hand on his holster, Gordon walked along a worn path that led through dry grass to the front steps. He tromped up the steps and onto the front porch, calling out, "Anyone home?" When he got to the open doorway, he motioned for the other two men to come forward.

When Henry got to the doorway, he took in the scene with a sweeping glance. Windsor was sitting on an old worn sofa with his elbows on his knees and his face in his hands. Gordon was standing to one side and looking down on him. At the far end of the sofa, an end table had been knocked over, and a kerosene lamp lay smashed on the floor. A small writing table stood pushed against the window, with loose papers scattered on the floor around it. A wooden chair lay on its back next to the table.

The sheriff's voice came out loud. "Who did this?"

Windsor raised his head to show a bruised and swollen face, but he did not look directly at anyone. The left eye was purple and nearly closed. "McCloud," he said. "The dirty sonofabitch McCloud."

The sheriff spoke again in the same demanding tone. "What did McCloud have to do with anything?"

"The man's a brute. A brutish sonofabitch."

"I asked you what he was doing here," snapped the sheriff.

Windsor moved his head slowly to look at the sheriff. "I could ask you the same question. What are you doing here?"

The sheriff folded his arms across his chest. "I came to ask questions. So I'll ask you one more time. What was McCloud doing here?"

Windsor covered his face again and spoke between the heels of his hands. "He beat me up. That's what."

"I can see that. I'm asking why."

"Money," Windsor groaned. "Stinking money that I didn't have."

"Money for what?"

"For his lovely black horses."

"Did you owe him money?"

"No, that little cur O'Leary owed him money. And he took it into his head that I must owe wages to O'Leary, so I should give the money to him."

"Did you owe money to O'Leary?"

Windsor looked up. "I should say not. He owed me. Plenty."

"Is that why you killed him?"

Windsor's face sagged and went blank, but he said nothing as he dropped his gaze.

The sheriff went on. "You killed O'Leary, and you can't deny it. You killed him because he owed you money, and worse, he was going to let it be known that you were trying to buy stolen calves. That's the truth, isn't it?"

Windsor's face was hidden again, and he remained silent. Henry looked at him, beaten and humiliated. Henry thought of McCloud, the dark avenger, taking his anger out on Windsor and helping O'Leary get even after all.

The sheriff spoke again, still in his authoritative tone. "You don't have to say anything. But you're under arrest. For the murder of Van O'Leary." The sheriff shifted his feet. "And for stealing this man's horse."

Windsor looked up. From the way his eyes widened, it seemed as if he were recognizing Henry for the first time.

Henry saw a change come over him. He was looking at a different Windsor—not just a bruised and disfigured Windsor, but a glassy-eyed Windsor whose face was smoldering in rage.

"You!" shouted Windsor. "You, of all people!" He pointed a shaking finger at arm's length.

"Me?"

"Yes, you! I accuse!" Windsor rose from the sofa, still pointing. "You took my money from O'Leary!"

The sheriff put his hand against Windsor's chest and had him sit down. Then he looked at Henry.

Henry looked Gordon square in the eyes. "I didn't take a cent. O'Leary offered me some money, but I didn't know where he got it, and I never took a cent."

The sheriff pushed out his lower lip and gave what might be half a nod.

Windsor raised his arm again. "You're a lying dog, just like O'Leary." Windsor's voice was quavering now. "You and O'Leary were thick as thieves, and you took the money and hid it."

"And so you took my horse?"

"You *owed* me! And if I had known where the money was, I would have done more than take a horse. You'd have gotten what you deserved, just like O'Leary." He gave a laugh in the bottom of his throat.

Henry thought about the cut ropes on his corral, the dead coyote hanging in his doorway. Then he recalled Molly tapping her head. Henry looked at the sheriff, and he could tell that the sheriff saw it just as clearly. The man was crazy.

The sheriff brought out a pair of handcuffs from his vest pocket. "Mr. Windsor," he said, "I'm also charging you with the theft of Henry Sommers's horse." He snapped the handcuffs onto Windsor's wrists and looked around. "You boys can wait outside while I search the place," he said. "I have a hunch I'll find the shotgun that he used to kill O'Leary."

Henry and Finch nodded and walked out onto the porch. Henry let out a long, low breath.

After a couple of minutes, the sheriff ushered Windsor onto the porch and closed the door behind him. He handed a double-barreled shotgun to Finch. "Hold this until I get him loaded up."

Henry looked at Windsor, who had smoothed out his clothes and had put on the clean hat. Outwardly, he looked almost as neat as always. In contrast, his bruised and swollen face gave him a tormented look, even though the glaze was gone from his eyes and the rage had apparently burned out.

In a calm voice, Windsor said, "I will be justified. You will see." Then he walked to the buckboard and climbed up to the seat, where he allowed the sheriff to run a small chain from the handcuffs to the front rail of the buckboard.

After stowing the shotgun, the sheriff pulled himself aboard and settled onto the seat next to Windsor. As he unwrapped the reins, he said, "Finch, I'll let you go get the horse. You boys can go on from there. I'll take this one back to town."

Henry glanced at Windsor, who was sitting straight up in his seat, with his chin and Vandyke slightly elevated. He was looking away from the other men, across a blank distance, as if he were snubbing them on the street.

When the buckboard had rolled away, Finch led Henry to a windmill about a half mile away, where a small pole corral stood screened off by a stand of young cottonwoods. Safe in the corral, nickering at the new arrivals, was the brown horse. Henry dismounted and crawled through the rails of the corral. He moved to the horse, patted him on the neck, and moved his hand on down the left shoulder and front leg. Then he brushed the horse's back with his open hand. Beau looked fine.

Henry turned to his fellow cowhand. "I thank you for this, Finch."

"My pleasure."

Henry fashioned a halter out of his rope, and they were ready to go. Leading Beau, he fell in alongside Finch on a leisurely ride back to Ruby Canyon.

Finch was clearly in a good mood. "I think McCloud helped out a little without knowing it," he said.

"How's that?"

"Softened Windsor up a little. By the time we got here he was so scared after McCloud's beating, he was just about glad to confess."

"Too bad for McCloud. He still lost out on his two horses."

"That he did. But I bet he got some satisfaction from thrashing Windsor."

"I imagine."

"And you can bet Windsor won't be stealing any horses for a while."

"I believe that."

Finch looked at Henry. "That was really a clumsy way of doing things, on his part."

Henry looked back and nodded. "I think, in the first place, he was just green when he threw in with O'Leary. New to the country and didn't know the rules out here. Of course none of that excuses his killing O'Leary or messing around with my belongings."

"Well, taking your horse sure helped him get hauled in." Finch twisted his mouth as he sniffed.

Henry said nothing. Finch wasn't quite smirking and gloating, but he was close to it. He was evidently pleased with the part he had played. Henry looked at Finch, and he felt he understood him. When bird-dogging O'Leary's young widow didn't work out, he got some satisfaction from tracking down O'Leary's murderer.

The next day being Sunday, Henry rented a buggy so he could drive Molly out to see her parents. As she walked out into the sunlight, she was wearing a tan dress and had a pink ribbon in her hair. Henry drove the buggy out of town in the freshness of the morning, when the sweet song of the meadowlark carried the best. As Ruby Canyon was not much out of the way, Henry drove to his homestead. Once there, he helped Molly down from the buggy, and the two of them stood together.

"It's pretty," said Molly. "All by itself, and the beautiful country all around."

"I sure like it. For a while there, it seemed like some of the joy had gone out of it. But I can feel it coming back."

Molly turned her eyes to him. "Yes, you're right. This place has a good feeling to it." She looked around at the cabin and the corral. "Where's the little black horse?"

"I took him into town with my own horse so I can go on to the ranch when we go back."

"That's good. But you could leave an animal here if you wanted, couldn't you?"

"I think so. If I was going to be around to take care of it." Then he realized she was asking about his sense of security. "I'll go back to leaving the place unlocked."

She looked around. "Do the deer come through here?"

"Not very often, but sometimes." He followed her gaze to the wild rose bushes, which looked weary now at mid-summer. "Wild roses," he said.

She nodded her head. After a moment's silence she turned around and said, "Do you need to get anything from your house?"

"No," he answered. "I left my bag in town with the horses."

She looked at him. "That reminds me. Did you ever use that thread?"

He smiled. "Yes, I did. One rainy day, I sewed up a rip in a shirt. It's packed away, but I'll show it to you one of these days."

Molly gave a light laugh. "How about the two bars of soap? Did you use them?"

He tried to suppress a smile as he recalled the two little packages so neatly wrapped. "No," he said, "Hollis the cook had plenty, so I'm saving them for later."

"For fall roundup?" Her eyes met his.

"No, for something after that." He moved toward her, and the last thing he saw before he closed his eyes was the pink ribbon and dark hair against a blue Wyoming sky.

Legend

**LOREN D. ESTLEMAN, ELMER KELTON,
JUDY ALTER, JAMES REASONER, JANE
CANDIA COLEMAN, ED GORMAN,
ROBERT J. RANDISI**

For the first time, these amazing talents—combined winners of 14 Spur Awards!—have joined forces, and the result is truly the stuff of legend. Together they recount the life of Lyle Speaks, from his hardscrabble boyhood in Texas to his later years as an aging cattle rancher in Montana, years in which his colorful past may yet come back to haunt him. From one end of the West to the other, Lyle's exploits made him famous—admired by some, feared by others. But now Lyle wants to set the record straight. No matter what the cost.

___4496-X $5.99 US/$6.99 CAN

**Dorchester Publishing Co., Inc.
P.O. Box 6640
Wayne, PA 19087-8640**

Please add $1.75 for shipping and handling for the first book and $.50 for each book thereafter. NY, NYC, and PA residents, please add appropriate sales tax. No cash, stamps, or C.O.D.s. All orders shipped within 6 weeks via postal service book rate. Canadian orders require $2.00 extra postage and must be paid in U.S. dollars through a U.S. banking facility.

Name_____
Address_____
City_____State_____Zip_____
I have enclosed $_____ in payment for the checked book(s).
Payment <u>must</u> accompany all orders. ❏ Please send a free catalog.
        CHECK OUT OUR WEBSITE! www.dorchesterpub.com

THE GALLOWSMAN

WILL CADE

Ben Woolard is a man ready to start over. The life he's leaving behind is filled with ghosts and pain. He lost his wife and children, and his career as a Union spy during the war still doesn't sit quite right with him, even if the man sent to the gallows by his testimony was a murderer. But now Ben's finally sobered up, moved west to Colorado, and put the past behind him. But sometimes the past just won't stay buried. And, as Ben learns when folks start telling him that the man he saw hanged is alive and in town—sometimes those ghosts come back.

___4452-8 $4.50 US/$5.50 CAN

TROUBLE MAN

ED GORMAN

Ray Coyle used to be a gunfighter. And when he gets word his boy has been killed in a gunfight in Coopersville, he has to go there—to bring the body home. But when the old gunfighter steps off the train, he brings his gun with him, along with something else . . . trouble.

___4440-4 $4.99 US/$5.99 CAN

HIGHPOCKETS

DOUGLAS SAVAGE

In the autumn of his days, Highpockets stumbles upon a half-frozen immigrant boy, nearly dead and terrified after being separated from his family's wagon train. For one long, brutal winter Highpockets tries to teach the boy all he needs to know to survive in a land as dangerous as it is beautiful. But will it be enough to see both man and boy through the deadly trial that is still to come?

___4400-5 $3.99 US/$4.99 CAN